Tales from the Jessica Files

TALES
FROM THE
JESSICA
FILES

After all, this is a love story.

PUNIS RUSSI

First printing edition 2022.

Published by Secret Freezer Publishing, LLC., PO Box 1025, El Mirage, Arizona, 85335

https://www.secretfreezerpublishing.com
https://punisrussi.me

ISBN: 979-8-9870842-1-2 (Paperback)
ISBN: 979-8-9870842-8-1 (Paperback)
ISBN: 979-8-9870842-7-4 (Hardcover)
ISBN: 979-8-9870842-2-9 (Hardcover)
ISBN: 979-8-9870842-3-6 (eBook)

Also by Punis Russi

Tales from the Jessica Files: The Companion Guide
Tales from the Jessica Files 2

This is for The Penguin, The Lion, and
the Shrimp.

Y'all my gatos and I will never, **EVER**, give
up my goal to write your story.

Table of Contents

Prologue

We were seated across from one another at a large round table. Typically, Jessica and I sat next to one another; she would ALWAYS be on my left, and I was always on the inside of wherever we sat. We loved being next to one another. She was a southpaw, and I was a normie right-hander. By doing this, we never worried about banging into one another. Well, at least not while we ate.

I smiled across the table at Jessica; I loved to look at her. I also loved the fuck out of her, so there was that too.

She mouthed to me, "I love you, Sir," or "Fuck off, be-otch." Ok, it was absolutely "I love you, Sir." The motions are nothing alike, I'm aware. It's called sarcasm, ass.

Jessica was so wonderful, not merely in her appearance, but her personality was her most outstanding feature. It made her so beautiful; she was just so astonishing.

She lit up a room, even at night, in the absence of any light or with a cloak of darkness on her.

It was her smile. It was just so bright and shiny. Her personality was so encompassing, so engaging. When we were together, the energy that we created multiplied. It was transformative.

She was just... mine. She was mine as I was hers, and not even eXXa could change that. Oh, how the spelling of her name annoyed the shit out of me.

I smiled at Jessica, gave her a little wink, and blew her a kiss.

She captured the kiss with her left hand and pulled it toward her chest. Towards her outside collar.

She clutched it, ever so innocuously and ever so
gently, but as she had many times in the past. I
don't believe she noticed me gazing at her doing so;
I'd have to look away to not make a spectacle over
it.

I was often disappointed when she grasped at her
ring, but I can say that I've never knowingly
commented about the move now that we have been
together for many, many years and on several
contracts.

There was something to it that presented as a
mental image to my mind, always knowing just how
much I meant to her, what our love meant to her,
and that the contract was incredibly important to
her.

She wasn't just along for the ride. No, she was all in.
Just as I was and just as we knew one another to be.
For life.

That necklace was something I had crafted for her, something no one else could or would ever have. It was unique, like her, and meant the world to me, like myself to her. She was just so amazing.

Sometimes I knew I was sitting across the table from nothingness when I did not have my Jessica. Those times were the harbinger of doom, the Albatross that would circle me like I was a Mariner, and this was my Rime.

I mouthed to her, "Ma'am, fancy yourself a quickie?" Only to get a finger-wagging and her mouthing the word "YOU!" towards me. Not even with a Sir, seriously? She knew she couldn't escape where we were, so perhaps...

And my phone vibrates. WTF? I look down, and it's my love of all loves calling me from across the table. Nah, 10 feet. No, really.

"Sir, if I were there right now, I'd bleep your bleep until we both bleeped, me at least twice. And you'd have loved it!"

My ever so witty trash talking ... "Grandma? Is that you calling me again?"

I laughed, and when I looked down at the phone, I realized Jessica had hung up on me. When I looked up, she was already scowling at me.

Oh, this shit was on.

I called her back. "Bitch! You know that was funny. You know this to be true!" I couldn't stop giggling—the tragedy of being a dumbass comedic idiot.

"Ma'am, I love you, through and through. You mean the world to me."

Jessica smiled back at me. That smile, that goddamn smile. The smile where I knew I was butter all over again. Damn it!

"Jessica, I'd bleep you on the table right now. I'd bleep you under the table! I'd break my bleep off in you bleeping you as hard as you know... oh shit; I didn't call my grandmother, did I?"

I looked at my phone, but nope. I looked up; Jessica had one of those smirks going on. It was adorable, so Jessica.

"Ma'am, I love you. More than anything in this life. You, just you. I love you."

I smiled while peering back at Jessica; she was beaming from pole to pole, knowing I had told her as much while in public.

I didn't need to be on the phone with her to say it, which was good.

And then, someone came over to me, asking me, "Punis, would you come up here and say a few things for the bride and groom? You are the best man, after all."

I winked at Jessica. She wasn't aware of what was going to happen. Goodness, for fuck's sake. I wasn't about to shit in the bride and groom's Cheerios, was I? Well, not for free, at least.

I walked up to the podium, vodka and smuggled-in Zevia in hand. I wanted this to be epic, loving, and touching.

"Maikel and Mishka, I have known you both for a lifetime. I introduced you to one another so many years ago. You are what people should aspire to be, to achieve."

"I won't toast you my toast, as it would seem out of season. I will say that if you love each other half as much as Jessica and I love one another, you will dunk on everyone's bitch ass."

I looked back to Maikel and Mishka; they were laughing their asses off. I spun around, and no one seemed off base. Was my fly undone? Nope. I can't imagine anyone got within range to touch me, let alone plant a sign on my back.

Nope, I can just be the life of the party if I so choose.

"I want to propose two toasts, one to Maikel and Mishka; may their reign be long and merciless. And to Jessica, I love you." I pointed around the room. "They all know this to be true."

That's how much I loved this woman. And I know she'd murdered anyone and everyone in the room for me. No, she wasn't a lunatic; she was my one, as I was hers.

There were no laughs, only the sound of awes. I glanced back at Jessica; I could see she was beaming once more. I stared and watched her mouth, "I love you more, Sir!"

Jessica smiled at me, gave me a little wink, and raised her hand towards her face, palm up. She blew me a return kiss.

I saw it coming. I did a Matrix-like move, catching it in the air to the ahhs of the crowd. I looked down at my closed palm with the kiss I caught in my right hand, bringing my hand to my chest.

All of this was in front of a crowd of roughly 150 people I did not know. Or gave a shit about. No, I cared about Jessica, none other. She was my one and only, my Ma'am, and I was her Sir.

Just because she got away with mouthing things to me without Sir tonight didn't mean she'd escape contract life.

No, she knew the game she was playing while out and about, and she knew I'd not punish her at this time for her violations.

I'd already been to The Other Side without her; I saw what would come to pass, and I wrote a book about it.

Jessica was extraordinary. And she was mine, mine and only mine!

———————————————————————————————

P1 - Entropy

Part one 1 of The Jessica Files. This week, we are introduced to this ridiculous couple and see what chicanery they get themselves into and how things get solved.

—-

I sat at my desk in the den, waiting patiently for Jessica to get home. I often found myself lost in my thoughts on Tuesday evenings since she worked a late shift at her day job. The rest of the time, it was a more standardized day shift.

I knew she would follow the same routine as any other day when Jessica got home. But Tuesdays were memorable for me because of Jessica's schedule; it allowed me to think out my plans with Jessica when she got home. My level of enthusiasm was higher due to that fact.

Jessica and I have been together for a while, and it has always been on long-term contracts from The Department of Rules and Contracts, or DORCs for short.

That worked for both of us as it provided a level of stability that we both craved.

Two cerebral introverts, and you'd think there'd be problems. Nope.

The contract was always super tight, expressing the limits of the relationship in clearly defined words and well-understood language. Setting those limits was paramount to such an endeavor's success, short-term or long-term.

I've been enthralled with her for a long time; she makes me smile just thinking about her. Her jovial nature towards me, her smile, and the beauty of her personage was remarkable and awe-inspiring.

Then as well as now.

Oh, plus she was super-hot as fuck.

I ensured that she took proper care of herself; we indicated that in the contract: nutrition and diet, mental and physical exercise, plus grooming at a top-notch level.

Jessica never indicated it to be an issue; if she did, she would have crossed off the appropriate lines in the contract we'd negotiated. Instead, she was always so eager when it came to renewal time.

That's one of the best aspects of contract life; every time it's up for renewal there was another chance to adjust the expectations. Luckily there's not been any changes over the last five contracts. Phew.

It's also fantastic for parties in the contract to be so happy with the terms that they are re-upped without even reviewing it. Jessica and I felt the same way with the words, a glossy, comfortable look in each of our own eyes.

It always makes me think back to the first time I saw her. God damn, she made my jaw drop when she looked over at me and gave me that smile. You know the smile, where you realize you are butter and being melted.

I didn't engage with her aside from shenanigans I'd pull while shopping, and our paths crossed. I so looked forward to that, but I never really let on that I intended to make her a part of my life.

And I did, and I am ever so fucking thankful for that Christmas Eve Day event. It was glorious. Jessica was stocking a refrigerated case and had turned around to get some more of whatever she was restocking.

She saw me out of the corner of her eye — she had told me a time or two — and proceeded to make a beeline to me. I wasn't expecting anything, to be honest, but the next five minutes changed both of our lives.

As she got closer, her smile got seemingly wider. Her cheeks had a slight flush look to them. And her eyes, well fuck, I don't know if I can express how I felt when I looked into her eyes.

What happened next was utterly unexpected. Jessica's arms started to reach out to me. I didn't know what the fuck was happening. I felt like a panic attack was coming on, not like that was anything new.

And then, Jessica hugged me. This was no pansy-ass hug; two humans' bodies pressed together in a non-sexual manner. I could feel her against me; it was transforming two into one.

We did that explorative dance with our eyes, darting from one focus point to another. I wished we had just kissed then in so many ways rather than waiting the next night, Christmas Night.

She was my gift from all that was above and below. She was the gift sent to ease, perhaps stop, all of my pain.

Jessica wasn't the solution; she was just a part of the puzzle that allowed me to become one with myself, my existence, all that is, and all that I will become.

Jessica made me a human again; we both knew and celebrated that. I owe her my life; I wouldn't have managed that in other timelines.

I am getting ahead of myself here. How uncommon of me.

After the hug that felt like an eternity, we stood in front of each other, not three feet – arm's length – apart. Jessica was taller than any other woman – if I recall correctly – I had been with.

I used to date tiny gals, the tiniest of gals that were five-foot-one-inch and 100 lbs, with a towel. Stuff like that had been my wheelhouse except for the odd bird Ms. J.

Oh, Ms. J was unique. Like none other that I've met. She was smart, fucking uber smart; she was a fucking medical doctor for the love of Zeus. And she was so much more—we'll save that for another day.

Jessica was five- foot- nine- and-a-half-inches, and I stood a mere five- foot-eleven-inches. Of course, I'm much more accustomed to a different frame. That did not matter because, at that moment, I changed.

That was the first of many changes that her presence had given me. She was so fantastic as a person; it made you want to be a better human because of that alone.

We were nearly at eye level, looking at one another as we had a conversation. It was the conversation you would remember because of its significance and yet forget everything as you were trapped inside your mind.

It was glorious. We discussed our holiday plans, whom we had in our lives, and the sadness we both held onto at the time. Family. Well, parents.

I won't divulge it here, but we both have our own shit, just like everyone else. Jessica made me believe she was trying to own it, and as we all know, I own my own shit.

That meandered the discussion into our holiday plans. I didn't have any, for I was on call for some stupid fucking reason. But then again, those clowns...

Jessica told me she didn't have any plans. Boom, a lightbulb for later. I could hear myself saying, "Hey, pay attention to her. Hindbrain's got the details."

Just as the conversation was getting to be rather interesting, the PA came on asking for all associates to go to the service desk. In some lives, I let her walk away; in others...

I stopped her as we parted and said, "By the way, my name is Punis. And you are?" as I gestured my hand for an introduction. In all this time, we'd never exchanged that.

She stopped in her tracks without my touch; she slowly spun around and spoke, "My name is Jessica, and it's my pleasure to meet you." With that, I was fucking sold.

I smiled at her and stated, "It's nice to meet you, Jessica. Say, since you don't have any plans tomorrow night, would you like to get together and talk about our fortunes?"

I don't think I'd even finished that sentence before she said, "Yes, I would like that. Give me your phone." And with that, she created a contact entry for herself.

I stared at Jessica, awash with feelings about another human I had not felt in a very, very long time–such a long time. And that made me very, very happy.

Jessica sent herself a text that said one word, "Punis." I felt like we were hooked on each other.

I felt like Phil Brooks in Chicago talking about feeling like Britt Baker in Pittsburg.

With that, she turned to walk away, only a step or two; she paused and turned around, clearly catching me staring at her ass. It's ok now as it was then.

And I don't have to say that because the contract favors me in this regard.

She paused and said, "I'll call you tonight, ok?"

There was no answer I could come up with other than, "Yes, Ma'am."

She looked at me as she turned and walk away, sashaying her ass as if she had just won the lottery, and she was riding the wave of emotions that came with it. She's told me as much a time or two.

I recall wondering if that was the end, like it had been with my friend "Andrea" from Florida. That ass walking away moment if you will. Hmm, I wonder if that'll catch on.

Once I had come back to earth, seemingly hours later, but in reality, just a few moments, I texted a friend of mine who was familiar with the Sapphire Chronicles.

She was enthusiastic for me but hesitant to be all in pending that following conversation. I agreed, but I felt I knew what would come to pass.

I told her, "Dana, this was it. For real. This was a win of epic proportions. With just a hug, I am hooked on a human I have respectfully admired from a safe distance."

Dana knew the quality of the person I was (and am), and she knew I wasn't about to change the integrity that I value so highly on something as dumb as a piece of ass.

No, Jessica was worth so much more than that now. In a blink of an eye, I heard the garage door open. And yes, her car had an interior parking spot next to mine.

I stood up, moved to the kitchen where she knew I'd be, and counted the paces of how long it typically took for her to come in. It wasn't bad or anything, just that I couldn't wait.

I heard the doorknob turning, knowing I would always have it unlocked for her. Except like two times, and you just heard a thud —typically when I was lost in my mind, thinking about her.

"Sir, I'm home!" she proclaimed as if I weren't waiting for her in our agreed-upon place.

As she entered the kitchen, I saw that beam in her eyes as I did many years ago on Christmas Eve. She was lit up like a Festivus pole or some shit.

Jessica put down her jacket and purse, where she was approved to do so. I just watched, amazed that this fantastic human was here for me.

"Sir? Shall I...?"

I looked and smiled, knowing that this would be one of my joys of the day. I paused as she came back around the kitchen island to me.

"Jessica, you shalt." And with that, she moved the anti-fatigue mat I had gotten her moons ago to a position in front of me. She knew the drill; she knew the routine.

Standing with her back to me, she bowed her head slightly with her hair pulled up. This was the part that I loved the most. Oh man. Just, oh man.

I gently reached over to her exposed neck and unhooked the clasp on her necklace, the one I had personally handcrafted for her from things of my past.

This was the way, I thought to myself. Sorry, no dopy Mandalorian shit here.

I pulled the necklace off, guiding it above her and then reclasping it.

She said, "Sir, would you put my inside collar on me, please?" And so I did—ahh, contracts, how they do things for all parties involved. Those DORCs are smart.

With her collar in place, I asked her quietly to please turn around. Then, I checked the fitment to ensure she wasn't being harmed; that's very important when doing shit like that.

I looked her in the eyes, staring into them as I had many years ago. I was in love with her as much now as I was then. Time had not changed any of it. But perhaps it made it sweeter.

It felt like 15 minutes, if only 30 seconds. I slowly grasped the well-placed protruding ring on her collar into my thumb and pointer finger.

The ritual we had, gave me great pleasure.

Jessica smiled at me; she always smiled at me, making me feel unique and essential to at least another human. Not just to my cats.

I pulled her close to me. She knew I'd never let harm come to her; that was in the contract we took so seriously.

She knew what was coming. We looked forward to it. It always started with a kiss like the first, full of love and hope. It never changed between us; that first kiss was memorable.

After that slow, tender kiss, I slowly released her from my grasp, knowing she knew the rules.

Jessica asked, "Sir, may I?" She was a veteran of the game; she knew the rituals and the decorum.

I replied, "You may."

She slid down her pants, doing the "no, these aren't too tight for me to wear" shuffle. Naturally, I took note of that as if I were going to change some part of her regimen.

I took the quick, fearful gaze back to be precisely that. I had to make sure Jessica knew the rules, and I was going to.

But she didn't need to lose any weight or exercise more. It wasn't anything like that. These types of things happen to adults as we age; you can't stop entropy.

Her pants were now down at her ankles; Jessica's eyes were fixed back on mine as she stood before me. It wasn't a showdown; she was waiting on my command.

I smirked and said, "Assume the position, Ma'am."
Jessica was instantly on all fours with her pants
down around her ankles while resting on the anti-
fatigue pad.

"Sir, I was bad today. I left the house without you,
and I accept the punishment that comes with it."

We both damn well knew she left the house for her
job, but it's a ritual we live by, and many others, in
the contract world.

I replied, "How many times were we bad, Ma'am?"

Jessica softly replied, as she always did, with some
arbitrary number of spanks she could take without
whimpering, even if Jessica knew she'd had
difficulty sitting later.

I used to think of her as a trooper, but as the years
passed, I knew she was a masochist. It was perfect
for me and part of why we were together. Not just in
the contract but because of absolute love.

Jessica replied, "Three?"

I laughed inwardly at her response like she was phishing for the correct number. Like always, I gave her a "Go fish...."

"Fine, four. But I don't know why I should have to chan...."

I slapped her ass hard enough that she knew to shut the fuck up.

"I'm sorry, Ma'am, but I cannot allow you to continue like that. You know the rules. You are not allowed to talk to me in such a manner. You should be so lucky not to get slapped in the face."

She knew I meant it, too, although it was something I never would do; I wouldn't raise my hand to her like that. I prayed I never would.

Sure, it's covered in the contract, but that doesn't allow me to abuse another person. Ever. Even if it's legal. Legal doesn't always mean right.

"Sir, I believe I deserve another four. Please ensure that I get all of them." I felt like I could have gotten an erection from that sentence alone.

"Get up, now!" I proclaimed in a fake aggressive voice. I could see the welts from my slap, so I knew she was all ears.

"Yes, Sir!" Quickly, she was back in front of me with her pants still around her ankles.

I let out a deep sigh.

"Jessica, do you believe in yourself that I love you?"

I hate saying shit like that, but there was a point.

Immediately she responded, "Yes, Sir. Absolutely, Sir. Since day one."

"Jessica, should I administer the rest of your discipline?"

Almost as quickly, she responded, "Yes, Sir. Absolutely, Sir."

I looked her deep in her eyes; I grabbed her by the ring on her collar, pulling her in towards me slightly and a bit more stiffly.

I asked, "Jessica, why should I continue with your discipline?"

And as quickly as the other two responses she had given, "Sir, I love you with all of my life. Whatever your decision is, I respect that, and I love you more."

How the fuck am I supposed to do my job when I have to contend with that?

"Jessica, thank you. Now... assume the position."

She did as I asked, albeit a little slower this time. I smirked at her. I knew the game I was playing.

I knew I wouldn't spank her again, even if she were due three more. Nope, not going to happen. I took a few steps to the side and opened the freezer to grab a gel ice pack I'd use for my knees.

Grabbing a clean dishtowel, I wrapped the ice pack with it and knelt next to Jessica. My face was adjacent to what was my swollen handprint on her ass.

I kissed where I had slapped her ass, gently and lovingly. It bothered me how things had gone this evening. It wasn't the first, and it wouldn't be the last.

I sat down on the mat while she remained on all fours. I did not say a word as I gently applied the ice pack to the swelling. She knew my compassion; I think that's another reason she loved me.

And we sat there for 15 min, with me rotating the icepack off and on every few minutes. All the while, Jessica stayed in her position. That was the actual punishment, you see.

I knew she would prefer to take the smacks to her ass than be made to sit there for however long I determined she should, knowing she was not supposed to move.

Like furniture.

————————————————————————————————

P2 - Sleep

Part two 2 of The Jessica Files. This week, we get caught up with Sir and Ma'am and see what chicanery they get themselves into and how things get solved.

—-

It was just another Tuesday, another day at home alone with the boys and wonderful cats: Fluffle, Shibby, and Tibor.

I work ten to twelve hours a day and usually get started before six in the morning.

I love the flexibility it has given me to do my job, writing about things that I find interesting. It feeds a part of my brain that I had suppressed during the vastness of my life.

I'll go into that later; right now, it's more important to focus on some other more pertinent facts to this aspect of our story.

Jessica did not get up with me in the morning. Nope, she got to sleep in late. We'd designed her schedule to allow her to work a short 10-2, just a couple of days per week.

I have knee problems, and sleep for me was often difficult. It may be something else in bed, but sleeping because of my knees isn't it.

I have long suspected, but I never bothered to ask Jessica about the three or four hours in the morning that she gets to have the bed to herself.

Is it the snoring? The shuddering of my body in pain? Was it the trips to the shower and back? Yeah, I'd rather not fucking know than poke at that shit.

In our candid moments or those "Off The Record" situations, Jessica had never complained or led me to believe the extra time in bed was an issue. I think I know why.

If you regularly slept with another person for whom you were sleeping incompatible for years, how would a couple of hours in the morning hurt? Am I right?

I'm saying that Jessica needs those extra couple of hours without me shitting in her cheerios whenever possible all night.

Not because she needs more sleep; she just needs better sleep. This leads to an exciting topic.

Jessica and I talked one night as I tossed and turned from the pain; she put her hand on my shoulder to help steady me more.

She slid in next to me and sweetly whispered, "I'm going to sleep in the guest room tonight. If I don't, I will murder your knees. And then where would we be?"

She was adorable. I loved that about her. She always found new ways to make me repeatedly fall in love with her. It was enrichening to my soul.

Jessica was the one that went to the guest room, not myself, who was the problem. And there was perfectly cromulent reasoning to it. Really.

It was in the contract. Yup, we negotiated some lines in the agreement a few years back. We got a nice bed for the guest room because of it.

Going to The Department of Rules and Contracts and seeing all the DORCs employees we'd become acquainted with was always fun.

She got to choose the bed, the size, the style, the sheets, the pillows, and basically everything! She knew she was the only one to sleep on it, aside from the occasional visitor.

I was not to sully her bed, and I initialed on that line without blinking. It was almost as important to me that she slept better than me, not in pain.

It's funny what kind of love and happiness can flourish between two people who were under a contract. I've never cared about anyone like I do Jessica; it's incredibly liberating.

I heard a sound –the whirring of the garage door as it lifted open, and you know what it means! Yes, I get to see my gal. It felt like it had been years since I'd seen her, and sometimes I believed it.

I went to my spot in the kitchen, waiting for our ritual. I had an "Oh, fuck!" moment when I realized I hadn't unlocked the door for her because I was lost in my mind. I was too late.

THUMP.

That's worthy of a facepalm. I thought about her so much that I didn't do my usual task.

"Sir? Could you get the door for me?" she asked. Oh, for fucks sake, dude, really now? My brain had already started in with me. Fucking with my every move.

"Yes, ma'am. On it," I shouted as I dashed to the door, jumping over one of the cats as if it were a rolling suitcase and I was OJ in an old rental car commercial.

I unlock the door to see the most beautiful human I have ever met, let alone loving in absolute, holding a clear coffee cup, the kind for Frappuccinos.

But it was just the cup because the Frappuccino was on her, and the whipped cream was on the ground.

She looked at me, somewhat stunned and unsure of what had just happened.

"Oh, fuck. Ma'am, I am very sorry," I said. Suddenly I had an idea—something to show my gal how I felt.

"Come here," I gestured with my arms out toward
her.

"Sir?" she asked with a confused tone. I imagine
she's wondering why I wanted to hug her, having
just dumped coffee on herself because of the door,
and then I could see she wasn't sure of the kind of
hug.

I didn't answer Jessica; I just went straight in for a
hug. A hug where my body was pressed against
hers, just like the Christmas Eve hug. That
spectacular hug.

And then I realized how cold the coffee was that I
had caused to spill, as I was feeling it against myself,
and my clothes were starting to absorb some of it.

As we stood there, like idiots, I kissed Jessica. Then,
I whispered to her, "Ma'am, let us go swap your
collar and get out of these wet clothes."

At that moment, Jessica realized why I hugged her
that way. She smirked at me, now knowing what my
intent was.

————————————————————————————————

P3 – Contracts

Part three 3 of The Jessica Files, Contracts. This week, we get caught up with Sir and Ma'am and the framework of contract life.

—-

Every day with Jessica is a treasure. I can't express how much I love her; I can't say how much I know she loves me. I know how she feels through actions, statements, and general intent.

She has signed many contracts with me as my love and subservient as I have done with her as her Dom. Without a doubt, we both know where the other stands on almost everything.

It's in the contract, stupid. Yup, it's a part of the DORCs standard contract.

Yes, that's a term that gets thrown around in this household. We used to find ourselves pulling out the thick document; umm yeah? "The DORCs Contract."

If it wasn't in there, we needed to negotiate.

And that is something we do from time to time.
Something would come up; we'd identify it. To the
contract, we'd go. Was it something that needed to
be amended? A new entry?

We'd negotiated so many times in the past that it
was so easy now. Fuck, Jessica and I had done so
many addendums that it was often a difficult time
to ensure that any changes or additions to the
standard contract were carried forward into the
next one.

But we always got it, Jessica and I. We always did.
Why? Love. And the threat of legal bullshit.

But mainly, it was respected. We were in this
together, legally, and we loved the fuck out of each
other. I can never recall a negative comment I've
ever made about her that wasn't directly to her.

And she would say the same, over and over, to me.
She was my "Ma'am," and I was her "Sir." I'd have it
no other way. I'd kill for her and defend her like
anyone who loved anything. And she'd do the same.

I know this because Jessica has staked her territory a time or two while not violent. Oh, how I loved that. Non-violent, stick her flag in me, fuck you bitches he's mine.

I'd look at her in awe, smiling, thinking, "How fucking lucky am I? How do I have such an amazing woman in my life? I am blessed. Also, she's mine. Mine!"

She was mine as I was hers. There were no third parties in this unless it was one of the cats—any of them.

She loved the boys, Fluffle, Shibby, and Tibor, as if they were hers, which warmed my heart with love. But like me, she loved the fuck out of Tibor. He was something very, very special. I've known this for a long time now.

She was everything. And I know I was her everything. I know this because she always followed the rituals and lived the rules, knowing both by heart. She was a lot smarter than most thought. Typical.

My Jessica was as devoted as you could imagine. When I said "jump," she said, "for how long, Sir?". She was a smart cookie, which made managing our lives easier. A lot!

That made ritual time so much more fun for me, exciting for her, and just a lot of fun that the average person would not see or comprehend. This lifestyle, living on contract, is a challenge.

You had expectations of the relationship, and.... you had the legal ones. The ones you agreed to with legal representation, notarized, and filed. That kind of love, if you will.

I can only tell my side of our relationship, but I never doubted from the hug till now that Jessica loved her "Sir." She was devoted to her "Sir." I can only lay this out in PG terms.

And I will do this as we progress, but I wanted to denote a few things that I've gotten mail about, about some of the contexts of the contract.

- Yes, it's called The Department of Rules and Contracts.
- Yes, she is to do what I say when I say so long as it is within the purview of the law and the contract. Note the order.
- Yes, anything and everything (legal speak).
- Yes, she is a fantastic cook in her skills. Jessica might as well have gone to the Culinary.
- Yes, she hated dusting the house as much as I did, and it was in the contract that neither of us was required to do so.
- Yes, we routinely play rock/paper/scissors to see who "got" to dust.
- And yes, she really has wanted to murder my knees. Sadly, on more than one occasion.

I am so thankful to have her in my life, and.... that brings us to today's topic. It's called "Do what I say, period." Yes, there are parts of contracts that we know exist but hope not to deal with.

I'm not talking about the "Clean the toilet with your tongue" type of stupidity. This tells someone what you want them to do in clear, concise language. Nope, it's more interesting.

As with the ritual of exchanging inside and outside collars, there are things that you are supposed to do in a relationship non-sexually and not in a slave-like manner.

Unless it's a Slave Leia thing.

Not like that doesn't happen every year on 5/4... Sorry, what was I saying? I got lost in an outfit I had bought her a few years ago, which could only be worn on that date.

I know that she loved that outfit because she worked hard whenever it came that time. She was never out of shape, but you can only be in that shape for a while.

For Jessica to do that meant so much to me; it was another sign of her dedication to the contract.

And speaking of wardrobe, I was always in control of what she wore. It was within my purview to approve or deny what she wore. Period.

I was able to set out what I wanted her to wear at whatever point I chose.

When we went out, I would specify what I wanted her to wear. When she left the house without me, I would select what I wanted her to wear. It was all in the contract.

We called this "**Fashion Runway Time**," and it was such a mixed bag. Sometimes it was one outfit; in others, they would end in a spank. Thusly blowing up the spot.

Bedtime garb, you ask? Well, that was a different story. I always left that up to her. Historically, when I was alone, I would sleep in basketball shorts. That was a knee thing.

But when I had her with me, I typically slept naked because I wanted to be next to her. I always wanted to be next to her and feel her against me. Can I say that in an incredibly non-sexual manner?

My job was to dictate her hairstyle, hair color, makeup, lipstick, and overall appearance. That was all my responsibility to take care of. Contract, yup.

I had to ensure that she had what I wanted and was sufficiently equipped for it. That was my job, and fuck, I loved it. And so did she. She got such a level of happiness; it was adorable.

There were many requirements that I had to take care of in this that most people miss. It was like having a child that you had to care for. And I don't care for children.

But wait, there was so much more. Respect was a big part of it. No, a vast amount of it. It was expected for Jessica to say "Please" and "may I?" and above and beyond, addressing me as "Sir."

There are a million and one different other things in the contract that we had to do. I didn't just get to sit back, enjoy a drink, and have some bimbo service me.

Nope, I had Jessica for that. Did she ever know how to make me a Cromulent Vodka/Zevia? Be it the regular (caffeine-free), the Ginger Ale, or the Lemon Lime, and she knew how to satisfy me.

Jessica always knew when it was time for a refill. She was observant, an excellent old-school housewife, and a fantastic human. And she is sexy as all fuck. And intelligent, damn, she is brilliant.

I'll close this week on this; the contract exists to protect all parties in an arrangement. Since The Department of Rules and Contracts exists, you must know it's a business agreement.

I've been trying to lay out some of the frameworks for the relationship, and in the next episode, I'll notate some examples of the contract in play.

———————————————————————————————

P4 - Dinner for Two

Part four 4 of The Jessica Files, Dinner for Two. This week, we get caught up with Sir and Ma'am and the framework of contract life.

—-

Jessica and I talked the other day, and she asked me nicely about going out to dinner. Who am I to tell such a fantastic gal as her that she would have to cook for the umpteenth night in a row?

Ok, it's not that bad. We go out from time to time. One of us will have a desire for something. We'll work together to find a place that meets our gastro needs, more mine than hers.

"Sir, I'd like to go for sit-down Chinese food at Hello Shen Go."

I loved it when she'd do that. She looked so her. So adorable. I wanted to kiss her when she did that, and that would happen.

"Ma'am, come here." Not too forcefully, but with a come hither for your best interest and gain tone. Yes, you can do that if you have a swagger. Or big balls.

"Yes, Sir." I always loved hearing her say it. Not as much as when we've been drinking pretty hard, and I say something like that to her, and in return, I'd get some Australian accent.

I never knew where it was coming from, and any time I'd ask, I would get some sort of shrug.

And that just made me want to hug her and kiss her more. Oh, how amazing was she.

But it always came with a price. There's a price for everything, and everyone's got a price. Just ask The Million Dollar Man, Ted DiBiase. The dude made bank there.

There was always the fun and the punishment, which was my fun. I never wanted to be mean, but I was always creative in steering Jessica in the relationship due to the contract.

Yeah, legally binding documents with the DORCs, were always beneficial. It also covered one or both parties' asses when it came down to it.

I tell you, contract life has TONS to offer.

So, I walked over to her, sitting at the kitchen table. I looked at her, smiled that shit-eating grin, and gently grasped the ring on her collar, giving it a very easy tug.

I mean to say it was half-assed and meant to inform her that she needed to stand up so I could address her. But, in this case, I wanted to plant a kiss on her because of the story.

I looked into Jessica's eyes, still smiling, and said, "Ma'am, we can go out to Hello Shen Go... if, and only if, you can give me a tender kiss to convince me."

Like, I wasn't fucking just wanting a kiss from my sub. It was as clear as transparent aluminum.

Jessica planted a lovely kiss on me like she always did. Jessica was mine, no one else's. And she knew there was always the pressure there to be the part.

She had bad days, even if they were few and far between. But then again, we all do.

Someday I'll talk about some of those bad days and what they brought about. It was never pretty, unlike Jessica. She was beautiful while at rest, during some passion, and even being ill.

And with that kiss, the deal was sealed. We were going to dinner. And Jessica was smart enough to give us a good 30-45 min head start. Why? Because it was wardrobe showoff time: contract, yup.

As I fluttered my eyes about, playing my part in this and thoroughly enjoying such a sweet-ass kiss, I said to her, "You know where you need to go," and pointed.

It wasn't towards my junk or the bed; it was to her closet. It was for her to start finding an outfit for dinner.

As she started to dash away, giddy like a schoolgirl, I reminded her of something significant...

"Ma'am, we require another drink refill before you start fashion runway time."

I smiled. Probably more like grinned from ear to fucking ear. Yes, not only could Jessica make a stellar drink, but she could cook a fantastic meal and bake a fucking chocolaty super yummy delectable treat.

"Yes, Sir. I will right now."

I kept grinning as she was something, all right. Jessica needed the structure and safety that our contract brought. It made her so much more whole as a person.

I got to see the transformation from Christmas Eve so many years ago. And you know, since the Christmas Night kiss, there's been only a couple of nights we didn't sleep together.

It was a spark, some ignition of ourselves. And this was before the first contract signing. We wanted to be in each other's company, such a particular emotion. So we did "it" for another.

And then I had a drink in hand. Jessica didn't take them to the brim as I did, but that's good since walking ten feet with one usually means cleaning up. And one day we'll talk about that.

I took a sip and smiled, "Ma'am, one more kiss before we start the show, please." I tried to say please even when I didn't need to—DORCs contract.

The Department of Rules and Contracts exists for a reason, right?

I received said kiss, both of us gleeful in it. I nodded in that direction, and she replied, "Yes, Sir." And she moved as quickly as her drink would let her.

I stood there in the kitchen, watching Jessica walk away. I felt like I was in another life; I watched her walk away from me in the store on Christmas Eve.

Never to see her again. A fate as painful as continuously stepping on a rusty nail with no tetanus shot to save me. It was insanity, for which I could not grasp or escape.

And as I contemplated such a horrible fate, out came Jessica in some hippy outfit complete with a weird ankle-length skirt. I shook my head and said, "Really?" It was so shitty that she didn't get a Ma'am.

I didn't want to return to that spot in my mind, but I couldn't stop it from taking over everything. It was like a liquid covering something so precious. Like oil from the Exxon Valdes.

A few minutes later, she came again wearing short shorts and a sleeveless top. I looked down slightly with a slight frown and nodded in disapproval. "I'm sorry, Sir, I will try harder!

"You better, or else, Ma'am." She knew that meant a spanking. Not the playful type, the one where I end up applying an icepack to her ass after however many failed outfits I had to endure.

And with that, she came out with a nice top and jeans combo. I think she could have been wearing that outfit when she left to get dressed; the spire of not having her was clouding me.

I nodded to her that it was good. "Can I fetch us a RydemNow, Ma'am?"

I got a nod, and we started another enjoyable evening together. Fuck, every bit of time with Jessica was like that, and I knew she felt like that toward me.

"Ma'am, come here so we can swap out your collar."
I loved this ritual, but not as much as Tuesday
evenings. Those were the best.

Jessica came to me, gave me a gentle kiss, and
turned around. I know she preferred her outdoor
collar, and why wouldn't she? It was amazing, like
her, and something she loved preciously, like me.

I won't say how, and I won't say "contract" because I
knew true love was there. I felt it in every kiss, every
spank, every time we were intimate.

You aren't with someone for years and feel like they
don't care, or maybe society is like that. Now, I've
put Jessica through many trials of faith from time
to time, and she's beaten them.

While not in the contract, I had built her outdoor
collar myself from jewelry that was mine, that I had
for dozens of years, and that held sentimental
value. When I gave it to her, I felt something
different.

But we'll save that for another day.

Once I had loosed and removed her inside collar, she was bare, in purgatory. She might as well have been at the DMV. I gently laid it around her neck and fastened it. Snug, but not a choker.

"Ma'am, had I known I'd get such an amazing cleavage view, I'd stand here longer."

"Sir, should we cancel the RydemNow and get take out? That way, we can have some time, then eat when you want us to eat?"

"Ma'am, while that was not my intent, that is an excellent idea. Since I haven't finished ordering the RydemNow, let's order via EatterGood."

"Sir, that's wonderful. Shall I go get changed?" I stared at her for a moment, confused by her statement.

"Ma'am, isn't there something you are forgetting?"

Jessica looked down and put one hand over her outdoor collar, gently holding it. I know she preferred it very much, but contracts exist for a reason.

"Yes, Sir, right away, Sir."

And with that, we changed out the collars. Of course, Jessica was less thrilled, but she was back to normal after a couple of seconds.

"Sir, what would you like me to wear?"

"Ma'am, I want you to wear the blue one that accentuates your breasts."

"Yes, Sir. May I get changed, Sir?"

"Yes, Ma'am, you may. I'll make us another round."

Another nod, and off she went. I smiled and put my phone away. Fuck ordering food; we were going to be playing for a while. I'll deal with that later.

———————————————————————————————

P5a - Bad

Part five 5 A of The Jessica Files, Bad. This week, we get caught up with Sir and Ma'am and the badness that even contract life can bring.

—-

I know this will sound strange, but even contracts can bring pain to all parties involved. Regardless of the party at fault, there is a fault that impacts the contract.

I've mentioned that I'd bring them up, and I have one for you, and I promise you will find it moderately not unacceptable. But why? Super simple. The meddling of outside forces.

Yup, even the great ones can be corrupted. It's a seed planted in the mind that grows into a shit show that is a relationship's poison. We've all been there as adults; I promise you that.

Some time ago, on a Tuesday, no less, a co-worker of Jessica's decided that she wanted to interject herself into the relationship.

This is during contract times with the backing of the DORCs.

It's not like her to come into the house and not follow the standardized routine. But that night, she did. She came in and put her stuff down in her usual spot. She was to go to me, but she walked past me.

This might sound petty, but in a contract situation, if you do not implement and follow the said contract, what is the reason for an arrangement? It's that fucking simple.

If I do not honor thou, why bother?

As she walked past me to the fridge, I stared at Jessica and then made herself a typical drink we'd have many of. She didn't even make me one. I stared even harder; she was making me exceedingly displeased.

I waited, expecting her to say, "OMG, my day was so bad, Sir. I'm sorry, but I needed this!"

I didn't get that. I got her looking at me. Not in the eyes, but looking at me.

"Ahem, are you forgetting yourself?"

No reply. What kind of shit ass badness is this?
WTF?

I paused, and then I walked over to her. I looked her
in her eyes, nearly nose to nose. I reached out, and
grabbed her outside collar firmly. She knew but
wasn't wavering.

I took a half step backward and broke her outside
collar off her neck, entirely into my hand. I
continued looking at her, knowing what would
come... nothing reasonable.

"Dude, what the fuck!?"

I took another half step backward, raised my hand,
and brought it towards my lips, gesturing for her to
be quiet. "Jessica, if you speak to me in that manner
again, I will be forced to Section 14 you." That
meant forced compliance.

She looked at me and said, "Dude, what the fuck!?".

I took another half step backward, took a deep breath, and forcefully stated, "I had told you in the past that if you ever fucking said that to me once again, your shit would be on the lawn as the locks are being changed."

Jessica paused, unsure if she was still playing an upper card. I've long wondered if it were her trying to remember what would be the consequences of a contractual negligent act, especially in regard to Section 14.

I continued to stare her down, angered. That is not something I would denote in our relationship; this was not normal. Something or someone had poisoned her mind, and now I had to give her the antidote.

"Now then, Jessica," I said with anger and annoyance, "Have I made myself clear? Or do you want to roll the dice?"

Again, Jessica paused, likely trying to calculate the odds, which was odd. She knew that she could never win. The contract was not in her favor here.

"I, I'm not sure this will work anymore. I think I need space..." she proclaimed.

WTF?

"You are in this, or get the fuck out of MY house." I pointed to the door. "Get the fuck out if you aren't all in."

No longer willing to fucking torture the shit out of my knees because some asshole bitchass person would pull this shit, I sighed and said something that I'd never imagined I would say to Jessica.

"Out. Out now, if you are not going to reply. And I'll fucking put your bitch ass outside myself, and you know I will. And you know it would be against my will and love for you."

Again, she paused.

"So be it." I entered her closet, grabbed as much clothing as possible, and walked to the front door. This was getting hard on me because I DID NOT, repeat, DID NOT want this.

I could see her starting to cave a little. But I continued. I unlocked the door, opened it, unlocked the security door *(cats related), and walked outside with roughly one-quarter of her clothing, depositing them on the lawn.

When I walked back in, Jessica had slid herself down the kitchen cabinets, and in a crumpled state, she'd gone from "I think I'm in control" to "oh shit, I might be fucked here."

I walked again to the closet and grabbed more of her clothing. I walked past her without saying a word, again depositing her shit in the front yard, roughly next to the first load.

I had to make it worser so she understood the magnitude of how much she had fucked up in the contract world and how much worse this could have gone. I was within my contractual rights to put my hands on her in a not-so-loving way.

I entered the kitchen and grabbed a large StuffEmFull garbage bag, the 26-gallon big shit kind. I walked past her again, not bothering to look or acknowledge her.

I went to her dresser, which she could see, and I started pulling everything out, drawer by drawer. Everything. It was on at this point, fuck. I will not put up with insubordination like this. Ever.

As I walked past her and towards the front door, she put her arm out to stop me. I walked right past it and went outside.

I didn't dump her clothes but just put the bag outside, next to her clothing from the other two trips.

I returned to the kitchen, got another StuffEmFull 26-gallon bag, and then made my way into the bedroom to her dresser and continued to empty it.

Again, it was on. This won't end well because of the contract, of course. The DORCs knew what they were doing.

Jessica got to her feet as I filled up the bag. And again, as I walked past her, she put her arm out to stop me. However, it was at my chest and not my shit-ass knees.

I paused. I turned to Jessica in prick mode and said, "Excuse you, you no longer live here."

And with that, she started to cry. That was only the third time she'd cried in our many years together. As I write this, I don't recall the first, but the second was at our first collar ceremony. I think we both did.

I put my arm out and slowly pushed hers down. I then proceeded to take the StuffEmFull garbage bag to the front yard. Set it down with the others, walked back into the kitchen, and got another StuffEmFull garbage bag.

As I walked past her, she grabbed me with a hug. A nice kind of hug, not malicious. I stopped, although my hindbrain said keep fucking going. Push this. Alas, that was not the intent.

"Yes, what do you want, asshole!" Man, it's been a while since I said something like that to my Jessica, the only person to have worn my collar, inside and out. I just loved her so much.

....crying... "I'm sorry...."

I interrupted her, "I'm sorry, what?"

"I'm, I'm... I'm sorry, Sir. This is all my fault."

"Ya don't say, Jessica." My anger over the situation increased as I played my role in this shit show.

Fully aware of the gravity of what had happened, Jessica turned to me with tears running down her face and said, "Sir, can I have my inside collar now?"—stumbling her way through it.

"Jessica, you don't live here anymore. You have no collar. I will file with The Department of Rules and Contracts shortly." Again, I was laying it on thick, playing my part in this.

"But Sir, please don't! I love you. You know I love you. You know I do. Inside and out. With all my fiber and being."

And I cut her off. "And here we are, with all that. Just bullshit now as best I can tell."

I was starting to enjoy the role of dickbag cop in this scene. I was going to ride the shit out of this to make a point that she felt inside and out.

"Sir, my inside collar, please. I'll explain, but my inside collar, please."

I turned to square up on her entirely. I stared at this magnificent woman I loved with every breath I had ever taken. I was still highly pissed off. There were consequences to our actions in the contract world.

"You need to earn it, Jessica. On your knees, now!" I said while trying not to giggle. This was going to be epic. I wanted to know what caused this bullshit, and I would find out.

But there's a punishment due. It says so in our DORCs contract.

And before I had finished that thought, she was kneeling there in front of me, looking up, all sad and upset. I knew what the punishment would be— cue sadistic internal laughing.

I moved on my belt, unhooking it. I was hoping she thought oral because that wasn't intentional. No, none of this was sexual. Perverse, maybe, but not sexual.

I slowly removed my belt, hoping the thought changed from oral to a whipping. It seems like oral would have been less worse, right?

"Jessica, take your shirt off. And then your bra." I was getting turned on if not for talking shit like this. Oh, the life of a Dom. "Now!" I demanded. And off it came.

I stared down at her as she looked up at me, not knowing what would happen. How bad this was going to be. I wasn't going to get some oral service with the front door open, was I? (The answer was no.)

I stood there for a moment staring down at her. I knelt in front of her, nose to nose. She was no longer crying, no tears, which was significant in my book. Oh, the topless love of my life.

"Jessica, will you ever do something like this again?"

"No, Sir, I'm sorry, Sir. Let me explain, Sir."

I stopped her with my hands, gently pulling her into my chest with a hug. She started to tear up again; I could feel it. I held her there as if to let her finish getting out how she fucked up royally.

I could have gotten an erection because I was having so much fun with this, embellishing within the contract and generalizing The Department of Rules and Contracts guidelines.

It was like watching wrestling. Or curling.

——

P5b - Worser

Part five 5 b of The Jessica Files, Worser. This week, we get caught up with Sir and Ma'am and the fallout from the badness.

—-

▐▌ Jessica, you know this will cost you dearly, right?"

"Yes, Sir. I know. I will accept whatever punishment I deserve. But please, put my inside collar on, please. Let me be yours, please, Sir. I'm so sorry, Sir, it'll never happen again."

I think that's what she said, muffled by my t-shirt and her being upset. Ahh, sweet-sweet-don't-have-to-beat.

I think she finally got it, but I wasn't ready to ease off yet. Oh, hell no. She had been incredibly disrespectful in the contract world, and I could have knocked all her teeth out if I had wanted to.

And we have a great dentist covered by the DORCs contracts; if I recall correctly, it was a 45% discount. (sarcasm)

As a note, my parents taught me this simple, practical life lesson, a moral value when I turned 13. **"Never put your hands on another person without their permission."** Yup, years later, contract.

I never liked to be mean or discipline Jessica at all. She was always in step with the contract. Sometimes I wondered if she knew it better than I did. But if she did, this would never have happened.

"Jessica, why in the fuck should I let you back in? Most of your shit is out there; maybe you should be tied to the fucking tree that I hate so god damn much that you wanted." Jebus, this was total bad cop territory.

"But Sir..."

"No, shut the fuck up. You know what, Jessica? I've got just the thing to shut you the fuck up...." You'd think I was talking about my junk, and she started to move there. I was holding back the giggles.

"No." I positioned my right hand to the back of her neck, firmly but not aggressively, grabbing ahold of her. It was something I would do to arrange her to where I wanted her whenever I wanted something. This was akin to grabbing the ring on her indoor collar that she did not have on.

She stopped. She didn't say a word. She was at ease, knowing I would never hurt her in this position, no matter how pissed off I was. I mean, disappearing a sub's body is a considerable amount of work, especially on a Tuesday.

OK, jokes aside, I held her there for a few seconds, just off my chest, as if she was going downtown. I slowly moved her to the position I wanted her in. Right in front of me. Eye to eye.

And then I kissed her. And I didn't let our lip lock stop. Her eyes closed, mine open and staring at her, giving another human a peaceful, loving, emotive kiss. Sweet and tender, like we would typically do.

I kept my eyes open to see if she'd cry. And she did, tears down her cheeks. I pulled back a second later. I wasn't mad or anything; I just knew that she knew.

"Jessica, if you want your indoor collar, you must get all your belongings from outside and put them away."

She stood and walked outside, still topless, and made several trips. She put her clothes away, nice, neat, and tidy like we liked our stuff.

In this, I transitioned from kneeling to seated on one of the anti-fatigue mats. While not for this, they were for shit like this. Trust me.

With everything back in place, she came back to where I was. She knelt at the time, still topless, not even on the pad. I just wasn't sure what would happen or the outcome.

I just sat there, waiting to hear anything she had to say. Would it be profound? Would I have to stop staring at her naked breasts? Great questions remained in this long-ass story.

"Sir, my collar, please? Pretty please?" It was cute. Oh, how I loved her.

"Jessica, turn around and lay up against me so I can hold you this last time."

I heard a gasp, and I shut that shit down immediately. "Now."

And so, she lay with my arms around her, my belly to her back. And I got to sit there and stare at her sweet ass rack. Ok, that part is meant as a joke.

She lay there up against me, my arms around her upper body. But seriously, she had fantastic Bs, evenly and well configured. I can't describe it without being graphic(er). She was my Leeloo Dallas.

Yeah, she's cosplayed that a time or two on request. Yummy.

Anyways, we lay there. I reached up to the counter and grabbed her inside collar. I wanted to see what her response would be. I'm not sure that she knew that I had done so.

I brought it down and laid it around her upper chest; she perked up but remained in her spot. I watched her hands at her side to ensure she didn't move.

And they remained there, never moving.

I slipped it around her neck and fastened it as usual, except I made it one notch tighter. This was the lesson to be taught here tonight, and it would be rough.

It was time to get down to business. Ugg. I can't say enough how much I did not want this. But the DORCs rules say so.

I put two fingers on the inside of the collar, on the back of her neck, with my thumb on the outside. I slowly started to turn my hand to tighten it. This was a test, and I think she knew it.

I turned it a little more, creating more and more pressure on the leather and tightening it more and more. No matter how much nominal pressure I put on her. She was being submissive, back to more normal.

But trust had been broken, so I had to break her in again. And that was a bad thing. Sigh. I didn't want to, but I had to ensure that shit like this would never happen again.

Instead, I'd held, touched, and played with her breasts rather than performing this test. As much as I liked testing her, she had stepped out of line here, and I was very displeased.

I could see the effects of the situation as I was monitoring things extensively as I slowly ratcheted up the pressure some more. And still, she kept her arms at her side, never flinching.

I was VERY uncomfortable with this, and I wanted to see if she would cave in before I did. I knew I was getting close to doing so myself. I tried to keep my feelings in check here; it was paramount.

I turned it some more, not yet at a complete turn. It was disturbing me, but she never moved to stop me. No large gasps for air. It was as if she was at peace and was coming back to me.

"Sir, I love you. More, please."

Where the fuck did that come from? I queried, "Excuse me? More please, what?"

"More, please, Sir."

I think she was calling my bluff. Fuck. Great, I was hoping we were almost finished, and I could go to bed. I did not want to get sick here; the nausea was ticking up rapidly.

"Jessica, do you want more of this, or would you like to sleep on the floor right as you are?"

"Both, Sir, whatever you decide, Sir, I will respect that. I love you, Sir. I was wrong, Sir; I hope you'll forgive me one day."

Damn, I can't argue with that response. I didn't want either, to be fair. I wanted to be lying in bed with her, both of us naked, me being the big spoon. That wasn't going to happen at this point.

I gave her a hard turn that surprised her, jolting her; I hoped and prayed that I would never hear about this again. I was now pissed at myself. Still, she did not move.

Oh great, I know I will have to disappear her body. Just kidding, she was okay, all things being equal.

"I love you, Jessica." I twisted a little more. I was ready to throw up, hopefully not on her. And then her left arm moved back towards me, and she tapped on my leg.

Had she done that to the right, hmmm? I'd have to continue. But she knew which knee to touch, even in distress.

I let go completely, and Jessica gasped for some air to get back to normal. She'd done very well, whereas I hadn't. I was shaking more than my tremors could ever do. I wanted to cry; I was that upset.

"Sir, I'm sorry, Sir. I couldn't breathe. Sir, forgive me for that. I love you, Sir. Please."

I sat her up and reconfigured her collar to its standard notch—such a magnificent human.

"Sir, may I sleep here tonight?"

I didn't know where here was; I was dazed by what I had just been forced to do to bring her into compliance. FUCK! After 10 seconds of horrible cussing in my mind, this went from bad to worser.

"Jessica, I want you to stand up and take the rest of your clothes off. I want you to go into the bedroom. I want you to get into bed, naked, and wait for me while laying on your back, arms crossed. Now, Jessica."

She sprang up, took off the rest of her clothes, and walked quickly and quietly to bed. I sat there, I could feel myself welling up, and the tears came out —many of them. I was so upset with this.

It was disconcerting, and I could feel it. My hands were shaking to the point where I couldn't move them. I was about to start bawling, but I could barely hold back, even with tears streaming out.

I got up, went to the freezer, grabbed the bottle of Cromulent Vodka, opened it up, popped out the flow control, and took a big fucking swig. That one was hard. The second and third were worse.

I waited. Fuck it; there's going to be a fourth.

I cleaned the rim with a Clorox wipe, put the flow control back in, put the bottle back into the freezer, and stood leaning against it with the tears finally subsiding. I went to the sink, unsure if I would throw up or wash my hands.

I stood there for what felt like 15 minutes, but I had no idea how long it was. I just stood there, facing the sink, frozen in the moment.

Once I defrosted myself, I started the water, still wondering what the outcome would be. I was still very nauseated, not from the vodka, I presume.

Washing my hands it would be. I used a paper towel to dry my face before using it on my hands. What if she saw that? I don't know that she ever saw any of this; I wanted her to but also didn't.

This would be hard, so I dropped the AC a couple of degrees as I walked towards and into the bedroom, knowing fully what I had to do to cement my dominance.

I got undressed and rolled into bed. I gently but forcefully said, "Jessica, face me. Now." And she complied. "Jessica, I love you." She gazed back at me, partially unsure of what would happen.

I grabbed the ring on her inside collar and slowly pulled her to me. I gave her a customary, loving kiss.

"Jessica, assume your position." That was funny to say. Guess no dinner and all of the vodka had put me at ease.

She turned over on her other side and scooted towards the middle of the bed. She knew that she was once again the little spoon.

"Good night, Jessica." I slid myself up against her. "I love you, Jessica."

"Sir, I love you more now than I ever have." There was a pause. "I'm, I'm... I'm sorry, Sir, for the badness I created. I hope you can forgive me someday, Sir."

I pulled her in closer; I kissed the back of her head ever so gently. I thought long and hard about what I wanted to say, the message I wanted to convey.

I whispered to her, "Yes, I will forgive you one day, Jessica. Now get some sleep. You have a big day tomorrow, what with all the sucking of my dick you'll be doing."

I giggled because that was silly. I kissed her head again and whispered, "Jessica, I love you." I took an extended pause as if I were going to sleep.

"Goodnight, Ma'am."

————————————————————————————————

PØ- Christmas Night

Part zero o of The Jessica Files. This week, we get caught up with Sir and Ma'am, their origin story, and how Christmas Night transpired. This night is what made this Sir and this Ma'am whom we read about today.

—-

The day before the events I will describe and share with you was Christmas Eve. This gal, Jessica, was someone whom I was attracted to from afar. I felt something.

We may have flirted some while she was at work, but nothing stood out as a problem or noticeable. But we both knew the little games we were playing. We knew.

I felt like I was walking on air after leaving the store that night, Christmas Eve, so many years ago. Here I was, this guy, going to be disappointed when I never heard from this gal again.

I wouldn't have been surprised either way, but I wanted to hear from her again, knowing that her word – her bond – meant something. As if I longed for that time when word = bond.

Perhaps the reality was that I just wanted to see her again. Seeing her smile made me feel like I was someone rather than another lifeless person in the horde.

Someone interesting and important enough to warrant her time, energy, effort, and love.

I was in the kitchen with Tibor that evening. He was still small and fluffy, yet, he was still a colossal asshole, as has been my experience with Ragdolls. More likely, he was just one of my whole family.

I recall talking with Tibor as he chased a ball around the kitchen, often leaving it next to me and patiently waiting for me to pick it up and throw it. He was a fetch kitty.

I had thrown Tibor's ball across the kitchen, perhaps some 15 ft from myself, and he charged off to retrieve it. And then... then things started to be less imaginary and more reality.

My phone rings, blaring the Futurama theme song. That tune, oh, that tone that wakes, bakes, and makes me feel at home. Fuck, how I love that show.

That tune led me to answer the phone, and it had to be her because if it weren't, I'd have to destroy the planet in my anger. I wanted that chance to have an honest conversation with Jessica.

She was extraordinary, not just for bringing life to my phone with a unique ringtone. The one I had waited for all evening, hoping to hear from her.

Jessica brought hope to a shit show world. No, I'm not talking about post-2020... We are pre that shit show, but still in a slightly smaller, less shitty show.

I know that I had felt she could be rather spectacular. My friend, Dana, who was fully aware of the goings-on, knew it could be extraordinary. But friends hope that for one another, that's love.

I never in my wildest imagination would have thought that Jessica would turn out to be who she is now, nor would I have imagined how things would go over the next 36 hours.

"Yo." My normal salutation. I loved the idea of a salutation of "Moshi Moshi," but not enough people knew what that meant.

"Hi Punis, it's Jessica"... with a slight pause ... "from the store?" Like it was a question? I'm guilty of stupidity, for I am human, and humans are particularly stupid.

"Hi Jessica, so glad to hear from you." I, too, paused, mostly because I wanted to make a joke about her existence, and at least I would have a phone number as an incoming. I hoped.

"How was the rest of your day?" That was the best I could get out. But, oh good lord, had I set a new record for how long till I cratered something?

"I'm so glad you asked. A little while after you had left, another gal I work with asked me about me hugging you. At first, I was worried as if I was in trouble, so I firmly stated, 'Stay back, bitch, that guy is mine!'"

I started laughing because that was so funny and ridiculous that she was already claiming me as hers. It's like someone walking up to someone in a bar and claiming them on contract.

"Punis, why are you laughing so much?" That... was a probing question. I could hear "Danger, Will Robinson, danger" in my head.

"I'm sorry, Jessica. I mean no disrespect. It was simultaneously adorable and sarcastic. I liked it very much. But..." My trademark long pause in a statement. "You'll have to kiss me before you can claim me."

Without delay, Jessica stated emphatically, "Dude, I'd plant one on your kisser if I were there with you right now!"

Before the contract, she could call me dude. I didn't particularly like people calling me by my given name; some sort of slang or nickname was the game I played in.

You get used to it in competitive sports. Too many Punis's, I tell you.

Well, she's undoubtedly bringing it. I may have miscalculated things here. And those instances are few and far between. But still, I wasn't about to give her the "Does this sound like a dial tone to you?" treatment.

"Jessica, please don't call me dude, dude." Again, the bad pause... "Have you heard of the band Scatterbrain, by chance?"

"OMG! Here Comes Trouble! Don't Call Me, Dude!" And then she stopped as if deflating from the context.

"Jessica, I'm so glad you know who they are. I have a cat named after 'Here Comes Trouble,' except his name is Fluffle because, well...." My hands were shaking all over, making them nearly unusable, like usual. Fucking tremors.

"...I wasn't about to let my ex name a cat Killer and another Trouble, now was I?"

I could hear Jessica chuckling about that; as silly as it would seem, it was accurate as fuck. It was on.

"So, tell me, Jessica, do you enjoy laughing at
ridiculous yet true-life events that bordered
somewhere between the absurd and The Scary
Door?"

"No. Fucking. Way! You watch Futurama too?"
That wasn't a question; that was calling someone
out. Strong style shit. And yet, so adorable was
Jessica. My essence had found another on the same
wavelength, equal to me.

Tibor was too. I kept throwing the ball for him in
different but easy-to-find places. And then it was
back at my feet.

"Perhaps, perhaps. If it's your thing, can you Top 5
that?" Now that was a bold challenge to most any
fan of anything. But nerds, we be nerds.

"Hmm, Punis. I believe I can." And did she ever.
"Season##Episode##" style. She knew her shit,
almost as much as I did, but I'd have jumped across
the table to kiss her if I were sitting there with her.
So unreal.

But the feeling was always there, the one where she wasn't. When she walked away, and I did not stop her, I didn't introduce myself, never seeing or talking to her again. The fate of sadness consumed me.

You know that empty, hollow, defeated feeling that would lay landmines in your mind and soul, forever making love fleeting, if not impossible—having lost so much and not gained a lesson.

I listened to Jessica's Top 5 and why she felt the way she did. I didn't interrupt; I asked small questions for clarification and always showed the utmost respect.

The kind of respect for someone you care about in some way or another. I call it "Be Cool To Each Other." Show love in untold but appropriate ways, like in the business world.

As time passed, so did the jokes, knowledge, and entertainment. It was fantastical, too real and unreal at the same time. It was something out of The Scary Door.

I won't lie; I was already way into Jessica. But she had something special about her, something I couldn't believe others hadn't garnered for themselves—lay claim to.

We must have been on the phone for 2 hours when my phone started to blow up from monitoring at work. Another mystery to putting someone new on-call during Christmas was beyond dumb.

But pay me a ton of money at that time, and like any person, I'd swap memory out of desktop computers with no ill will. Try to hire me like that, and you can suck my balls.

"Jessica, I'm sure you can hear my phone blowing up; it's my mysteriously named 'day job'. I mean no disrespect, but would you still like to make plans for tomorrow?"

"Dude! Totally. I don't think I've ever had a conversation with someone this long. I'd very much like to see you again."

"Ahem, the song previously mentioned."

"Oh, shoot. I'm very sorry. What would you like me to call you? I'd very much respect that."

"Well, Ma'am... If you called me Sir, I'd much like that."

"If you call me Ma'am, deal!"

"That's a deal, Ma'am."

And with that, our monikers had been finalized. Without a first date, a first kiss, or a first time. Now there was a song that I both loved and hated.

"Ma'am, I do need to attend to work. If you are still interested in going out tomorrow, text me, and we'll make plans. You are my single point of interest."

"Sir, I don't care what we do, but please be with me to do it?"

God damn, was she amazing? "Ma'am, I'd only like to be with you or my cats. But, as far as I know, you can't," classic me, "use your tongue like that."

Such a dumb statement, but made with much sarcasm. I was pushing to find the edge, not to fuck things up beyond repair. Also, classic this guy.

"Ma'am, are we amenable?"

"Yes, Sir. I'd very much like to see you again, Sir."

And with that, I finished the call and went to deal with that shit show of work hell.

After dealing with the shit show work, I spent the rest of the night thinking about Jessica. I thought about every word I could recall hearing, every word I had said. She was foremost in my mind.

——

We went for dinner at a wonderful Mom and Pop Chinese food place, Hello Shen Go, which would later become a favorite of ours. The food was delicious; the atmosphere was delightful. It always was.

After dinner, after many hours of talking, eating, drinking, smiling, laughing, giggling, and being silly, it was time to go. I knew it was something neither of us wanted.

Jessica and I were standing outside together, nose to nose, and I said to her, "You're either going to kill me right now, or you're gonna put your hands on my shoulders and kiss me."

She put her hands on my shoulders, looked me dead in my eyes, and said, "I love you already."

After the shock of her profession, I noticed that Jessica had put her head on my shoulder while sliding her hands onto my back, silently standing with me against me.

It was so uniquely strange. But I stood there, my hands around Jessica's rib cage, wondering what would happen because I didn't sense that she had any weapons to hurt me except her love.

I waited until she came back around, squaring up to me, and I queried her, "I'm sorry, I didn't understand what you said. Could you repeat that, please?"

She looked deep into my eyes, probing back and forth like what had happened the night before and what would happen a million times more in our time together.

Then, finally, we just looked at each other dumbfounded, amazed, and perplexed.

She repeated, "I love you, Sir. I'm sorry if I was stuttering."

"You didn't stutter, Ma'am; I just wanted to hear you repeat it because it is a wonderful statement from a wonderful human who also happens to be hot as fuck."

"Hot as fuck?"

"Yes, Ma'am. As fuck."

I paused for what felt like an eternity.

"I want to love you, and only you and the cats: no one else, just you, Jessica. I'm not there yet, but I know that I will be. Be there with you; I want to be there with you."

I paused briefly. "So please don't stop or change your feelings; I just need a little extra time."

She gazed at me more. She slowly moved forward and planted a sweet and tender kiss on me that got me aroused without intent. I had to rotate a little bit as I didn't want to disappoint her yet.

And that was our first kiss. Jessica had already professed her love for me before even the intimacy of a kiss. A kiss. Sure, I had all kinds of wacky thoughts going through my head.

But then again, at this point, I can tell you that it never felt wrong. It always felt like it was supposed to be. So in this reality and infinitely more, Jessica and I were together.

But as time progressed, I would start seeing in my mind different realities where I watched her walk away from me, and I never got my Jessica.

I meant that the two of us ended up in bitter disappointment without each other. I saw it. I watched it. I lived it. I am it. This is fucking unreal.

And yet, I am standing here with the woman I will love through and through, the one to be mine as I am hers. She was "her," that one. The one. Not Jet Li's, The One.

She was consistent in all the realities I could see, feel, or perceive.

She was just everything. I had known that I loved her before Christmas Eve, but where would I be if I let on to that and didn't hold onto myself? We've all been hurt.

Some more than others. Most different than the rest. We all have our scars, inside and out; how we love another as a friend is what shows the goodness of humanity.

And all of this while staring into the Eyes Of A Stranger.

————————————————————————————————

P6 - Travel?

Part six 6 of The Jessica Files, Travel. This week, we get caught up with Sir and Ma'am and the distance of travel they have to endure, even more than contract life.

—-

Some love to travel, some dislike having to travel, and those like Jessica and I want to slap you for bringing it up. Travel was the worst for this duo.

Cars, meh. Anything else, middle finger. And that's what Jessica thought. My opinions were far worse about travel. I just wanted to be with Jessica, and I know she just wanted to be with her Sir.

However, many years on, we are now in the contract world, with the DORCs, to make sure contracts were adhered to, but mandatory travel?

Shit Show Earth decided to piss on the world again, but I had a gigantic umbrella because I got my gal. The one and only, my Jessica. I can't say how much I loved her; it would be sickening.

A few years ago, the DORCs added a provision on all new and renewing contracts requiring them to travel five business days per year, or more, outside their locale.

Those DORCs, what will they scheme up next?

We both had objected to the line in the contract, working with one's lawyers to find a way out of it.

Alas, it was that or dealt with a FULL audit by the DORCs. That was lame.

So, Jessica and I sat down one evening to discuss it.

"But, Sir, I don't want to leave home. Fuck the contract, Sir. I want to be here with the boys like you do." The boys are Fluffle, Shibby, and Tibor.

"I know, Ma'am. I'd instead do the same. I also don't want to deal with a DORC audit, you know? I let you slide on things in the contract, and if they check the books, we both will suffer."

I am unwilling to let anyone, any entity, between my Ma'am and me. So fuck, we have to travel. Those fucking DORCs!

It wasn't the first, nor would it be the last, time that the DORCs had caused problems in ANY relationship, including ours. Another day, it makes me too hot to get all riled up.

"Ma'am, where'd you like to go for a week this summer?"

"Sir, can we go to Mexico again? Playa Del Carma? Please, sir, that would be so wonderful, Sir." She stared at me; I felt sad about what I'd say next for us.

"Ma'am, travel to that part of the world is temporarily closed; we can't go there." I felt even sadder because we both loved the all-inclusive vacation life, drink/sleep/copulate, repeat.

"Ma'am, would there be anywhere in the US you'd want to go, aware of the heat here in Phoenix during the summer?" I felt somber, nah, deflated, asking that. I wanted the all-inclusive too.

"Sir, I can't say." She suddenly went quiet.

"Ahem, Ma'am, I asked you a question because I was interested in your opinion. And I would still like it."

She swung her head around towards me, stunned at my statement. She shouldn't have been, but I think it was the timing and tone. I didn't want to fuck around with the DORCs.

I wanted to fuck around with my Jessica, perhaps later if she turned things around. And yes, short straw in the contract world. You know your role and your responsibilities. Rarely should there be a surprise.

"But Sir, I wouldn't begin to know...."

I stopped her. "Jessica," man, I hate doing that, "I asked you a direct question. You are not answering it. You know the price, right?" Oh, she knew the price.

She knew it so much that she stood up, walked around the table in front of me, reached out and gave me a tender kiss, stood back up, slid her pants down, and got on all fours.

Fucking furniture, I tell you.

"Jessica?"

"Sir, I cannot answer your question and do not wish to anger you; I accept your discipline, however you see fit."

Fuck, right to the point. What was she trying to avoid? Hmm. Maybe a fingerprint or two will help her memory.

And with that, right palm left butt cheek. (TWACK) Her only movement was the force I put into it and my starting position.

She winced a little. And yet, she repeated, "Sir, I cannot answer your question and do not wish to anger you; I accept your discipline, however you see fit."

"Jessica, did you want to play the game of how much your ass can handle from me?" I started laughing aloud; that was funny.

"Sorry, that was funny. Jessica, do you want to play this game? You have never won; you can never win this one."

Again, "Sir, I cannot answer your question and do not wish to anger you; I accept your discipline, however you see fit."

Ok, fine. A second slap on the ass, in nearly the same spot. Like other times, I did not want this to escalate. I just wanted to know where she wanted to go. For fuck sake!

"Jessica, before I just go to town with your ass," the chuckling again, "because I love you, and I respect you as my Ma'am, before I rain down ten slaps in procession, in the same spot, do you want to say something?"

"Sir, I cannot...."

"Jessica, you are pissing me off. Stand up, pull your pants up, and kneel before Zod!" I giggled after saying that one; it's been a while since I used it.

"Yes, Sir."

And yes, I know that kneeling in jeans was more punishment than not wearing clothing. That's why I did it. I did not want to spank her more; I wanted my Jessica.

"Jessica, what in the holy hell? You have never acted like this about travel. Dude!"

"Sir, I'm sorry, Sir. I... I... I don't want to leave here."

"Ma'am, you do many times a week. I'm confused."

"But, Sir, I love it here. I don't want to be anywhere other than with you. You are my one and only Sir. I only wish to be with you, Sir."

Hmm, something strange was afoot at the Circle K.

"Jessica, I do not understand what the issue is. Would you kindly tell me? I am curious and concerned."

"Sir, I don't want to leave here."

"Jessica, what is the matter?"

"Punis, I love you, Sir, or not. I do not wish to be without you, ever and at all."

Wow, this was new. I can't recall the last time she called me by my given name. DORCs would say, "Up to a black eye, no further." I'd say none of that.

"Sweetie, please. Come here and sit here with me."
Something else that was not said very often.

Jessica sat down with me; I gently brushed her hair
back from her face before fake choking her with my
hands, like in a bad wrestling spot. She was
unfazed.

"Jessica, what's on your mind? I grant you off the
record."

"I'm afraid you'll have replaced me when I return if I
leave you. I don't want to be without you, Sir. You
are everything. I love you as a human, my Sir, and
my soulmate."

I felt like I would be the one starting to cry here.
That was so sweet and loving; my mind just went
blank.

"Sir, are you OK?"

"Sweetie, I love you. I waited a lifetime to meet you,
I waited a lifetime to hold you, and I waited a
lifetime for you to be mine. I cannot replace you,
nor could I upgrade from you.

"Jessica, you are everything I have ever wanted in my entire life. You are the greatest gift to me, greater than all the boys, greater than anything. You are my soulmate."

Now that was a BIG statement. All of the boys combined! Holy fuck, that was a strong statement.

"And Jessica, I've known that since Christmas Eve."

"Sir..." There was a bit of a delay as if she was unsure what to say. "You love me?"

"Bitch!" I giggled; it was silly to say. "Yes, Jessica, I could not imagine a world without you. I've seen the other side of Christmas Eve; it ends in many disappointments. For both of us."

That other side, that other fucking side. I've watched her walk away from me a million times, if not once, and it ends in so much misery for both of us; it's my wide-awake nightmare.

At first, I grabbed the back of her collar, so she knew, then slowly and gently pulled her back so I could catch the ring on the front. Once I had access to that, I would line her up for a shot.

And she fucking deserved that shot. Right on the kisser. With mine. And I let go of the ring and pulled her into me, nearly falling to the floor like morons. Or idiots in love.

"Jessica, I don't want to vacation without you; I never want to be without you. I want to know where you'd like to go on vacation, just the two of us."

She gently laid her arms around my shoulders and put her forehead on my shoulder, just like on Christmas night so many years ago.

Jessica paused as she would do from time to time.

"Sir? Could we go to Death Valley, California, together?"

I smiled in a way that only Jessica could make me smile. I wanted to kiss her. I wanted to ask her if those spanks had gone to her head and why she would ask to go there.

————————————————————————————————

P7 - Scared

Part seven 7 of The Jessica Files, Scared. This week, we get caught up with Sir and Ma'am and the scars that bind them, even more than contract life.

—-

If there was one thing that scared Jessica, it was my tremors. We found that they were worse in the morning than in the evening but, based on research, some of the medications I took were at the root cause, not just themselves but combined.

Jessica realized that we needed to see a neurologist as she continued to observe that I couldn't do simple tasks like holding something in one hand and trying to use a screwdriver simultaneously.

Typically, I'd have blown it off and said I was okay. That's a very standardized male defensive tactic. The Man Manual has an extensive amount of data there to support that.

I didn't have the ability or the stability to perform simple tasks. Trying to hold something in one hand and using a screwdriver in the other was brutally difficult, often featuring me loudly exclaiming, "FUCK!"

It was saddening and hard for her at first, but she had told me straight up that it scared her.

And frankly, it did scare the fuck out of me, and that's not just because of my relationship with Jessica and the contract but because I worried about the long-term effects of five concussions from many years of competitive sports.

I knew I would never be able to take care of myself. That the neurological damage from that many concussions was a huge problem.

And this isn't meant as a downer; this is a story about how Jessica has dealt with my issues and how amazing of a human she is. She has never shied away from helping me.

And that is because she is the greatest thing in my world, more so than any of the boys, Fluffle, Shibby, and Tibor.

She means everything to me, helps me take care of myself, and brings me so much, love.

The most impressive part of this fact is that she is NOT obligated at all, or in any way, to take care of the vast majority of the physical ailments I am suffering from.

She does so out of pure love, and she is the first human I would, without question, do the same. She is astonishing.

The funny thing is that, on our Christmas Night date, how we put our hands on the table in a show of good faith as we had a conversation about personal things.

Jessica could see my hand shaking at first. She asked if I was nervous, and I responded honestly with yes. Why do you ask? She commented about my hands shaking.

I casually replied, "Oh, that's not nerves." Talk about harbingers...

Then after many drinks, my shakes were gone.

As the night went on into the morning, she could start fueling my tremors. That's not a sexual joke; it's about neurological issues in my hands. Although I always wondered...

We were in bed; she had just woken up. She turned over to me and said in a groggy voice, "Who the fuck are you?"

I chuckled.

"Are you OK? I can feel you're trembling. No, that's not a sexual joke."

I couldn't contain my giggling. "I'm fine...." and the giggling stopped, "but I didn't have my sleeping medications, so I didn't sleep."

"You didn't sleep well?"

I once again replied, "I didn't sleep."

She rolled completely over from where she was in the little spoon, squared up to my face, nose to nose. Our eyes probed each other again, like two nights before, at the store.

"Do you want to be with me, long term?" she asked.

In my mind, I said, "Do you like to drink heavily, smoke a ton of pot, watch cartoons, and have a lot of sex?"

And what I said out loud was, after a 3-4 second delay. "Do you like to drink heavily, smoke a ton of pot, watch cartoons, and have a lot of sex?"

Oh fuck, what did I just do? Damn it, dude!

As we lay there, she took hold of my hands, slowly and gently massaging them to ease the pain of the tremors, now able to feel them for herself. She stayed engaged with my eyes, staring contently into mine.

She smiled; she smiled that smile that melts the will of good men and evil men. "I'd be scared about your hands, but I know I do when they are in mine."

I lay there stunned, not sure what exactly Jessica had said. Was that a haiku? Did it mean that she wanted something long-term? What the hell, human!

Later that morning, the tremors were there, and she was too. While not having been intimate, we spent the night together. That was an excellent start to what we have built.

And I think that that was the first glimpse into the physical problems I have for her, and yet, here we are so many years later, and she is still by my side as I am by hers.

I can only hope that as time progresses, I can count on her to continue taking care of me, as she has been for a long time, but there is never a day that I look at her, and I go, who are you?

That would be a level of pain that I know many have suffered from a loved one. That would be the day my soul died for good.

This was serious and something I was scared of dealing with myself.

It is often hard to articulate to the uninitiated folk who haven't dealt with certain types of illnesses.

While my issues have developed some before Jessica, more so with her, it shows how wonderful she is, how she has cared for me and allowed me to care for her.

Jessica has never shied away from the fact that she will have to take care of me, given our age difference; adding this on top is another layer to the scared cake that we bake. Stoner thing.

As I write this, it is the 20th of April, and there's a good amount of baking that Jessica and I have done all day. Plus, we had Futurama on non-stop.

By being under contract and loving her absolutely and how I know that she loves me the same, she is the first person I'd ever say that if she were disabled that I would take care of her, and you can bet your fucking ass that is not in the contract.

———————————————————————————————————————

P8 - Testing

Part eight 8 of The Jessica Files, Testing. This week, we get caught up with Sir and Ma'am and the tests that bind them, even more than contract life.

—-

You could go to City Hall, sign a piece of paper, and you could walk away whenever you wanted, although there was typically a financial penalty, as most have experienced.

Or you could pledge yourself to another in a legally binding contractual agreement. This is a severe endeavor between two consenting adults, and how much more invasive the governing body is as they are required to uphold a contract.

I will also try to detail a lot of the process and what it was like for me, the painfulness given my real-life conditions: privacy, knees, medications, and things of that nature. Own your own shit, right?

Ultimately, the question that everyone wants to know... How much love do I have for this person to put me through that, and if this is what I'm willing to do for Jessica, what is she willing to do for me?

Every time contract renewals came around, Jessica and I were required to undergo various tests to ensure that we were fit and adequately suited to perform the duties of the contract.

And like in various professional sports, you had rigorous testing by the Department of Rules and Contracts, or DORCs, which was an exceptional level in Dante's Inferno.

Per the DORCs, contracts are considered absolute, and there are no divorces, separations, or breakups from a contract. You are not required to be in a contract with somebody, and the DORCs have made that extremely clear.

Should you wish to have an ongoing relationship that provides the security of a contract and the life it can bring, you must go through an intensive and invasive process.

Why? Because you have to represent yourself accurately and provide particular assurances to the other party before finalizing the contract.

The DORCs are the arbitrators and final judges of all contract-related issues, and their rule is absolute. They are the folks in charge, those DORCs, because this is a contract world.

I generally had no issue with the contracts and their testing requirements; I knew they were an integral part of the process and necessary to ensure that one accurately represented oneself.

That sounds like a repeat, but it is important. While contract rules are slightly different, coming out of a contract and going into another was a different story.

The testing there was much, much more excruciatingly painful.

I don't know how much detail I can go into without the DORCs being pissed off at me, but I do mean that it is similar to a professional sports contract signing and the rigorous testing that is required.

This is not only psychological and physical testing but also genetic background tests and conversations with people familiar with them going back to their childhood, like a Top Secret Clearance.

Do you want to ensure you're not getting damaged goods if you spend $250 million on a professional athlete?

And why would I, as a Dom, want to engage in business with somebody who is damaged goods?

And I don't mean from a psychological standpoint because I might consider myself as damaged goods.

While I never perceived Jessica as that in this regard, she was damaged. And so was I. But who in the contract world wasn't? I can't go into Jessica's damage because I'm not a psychiatrist, psychologist, or practicing doctor.

I'm the man who takes care of this woman who follows a series of rules, like myself, in a world where pre-contract testing and yearly reviews occur. And I'll cover "Reviews" in another chapter.

I can't dictate what it was like for Jessica before our first contract signing and everything she had to go through.

I can say that what I went through was very invasive and emotionally painful because they were required to dredge up that level of information to ensure that I've best accurately represented myself.

And they held Jessica to the same standard as anybody signing a contract. The one thing that we could say about the DORCs is that they were exceptionally thorough because they were a government entity.

Sadly, we all know the government; those motherfuckers aren't here to make our lives easy. But you know this, and you know that anytime you deal with the government, not a good time.

I remember going to the central bureaucracy and meeting the DORCs for the first time. While they were cordial and nonthreatening at first, I realized how painful they would make things for both of us.

Since the Department of Rules and Contracts exists, they have absolute power over contract-related relationships.

Much like we saw with their change to the travel policy, they could change rules and regulations as they saw fit to best accurately represent all of the members of the DORCs.

Mind you, changes were not arbitrary and done on a whim to fuck somebody over, but they often required going to one's legal counsel and spending money on something you shouldn't have to.

It wasn't just said I had to do it; Jessica had to do it with her legal counsel.

Paying two different law firms to tell me I was fucked was difficult, and when spending much time thinking about it, it was completely irrational.

I would do that for Jessica in a heartbeat because of my love for her as a human and as the love of my life.

When I walked into the DORCs for the first time
and went to the front desk, I conversed with the
receptionist to understand where I needed to go
and how I knew shit was on.

I never felt like it was wrong. It always felt like it was
supposed to be this way, that there would never be
a different way from this. This is how it was
supposed to be because this is what Jessica and I
were.

I remember going into what would be the
equivalent of a doctor's office, and in talking to the
on-staff physician, they asked me a ridiculous
number of questions.

- My complete medical history,
- Any medications that I took,
- All of the supplements that I took,
- My height, weight, and BMI.

It had no level of privacy. And I mean no level. After
the 2 1/2 hour thorough examination that did not
include a proctology exam, I'm sure they would've
done that if I'd had asked, and they'd have used
Captain Hook's hand.

I knew I could be the person I believed I was and take care of Jessica for the woman she is and my immense love for her.

Jessica had no problem when I brought up asking her to wear my collar, inside and out. I think that she knew that that was what she wanted and that I was with whom she wanted to share that lifestyle.

And there was nobody else I would have or would like to wear my collar, inside and out.

With the collar, there was an inside and out version. The inside version was typically a thicker, more leather material neckpiece similar to what you would see on a dog or some chick at a rave.

Except it didn't include a pacifier.

Inside collars were designed for behind closed doors and were much more private and intimate.

However, an outside collar was more about presentation and function to ensure that other people could recognize that you wore someone's collar.

In my case, I constructed Jessica's collar by hand from things in my past that meant something to me.

In our case, it was a sterling silver chain and a ring that I used to wear on my right hand, pinkie, not a wedding ring, put together so that it sat high up on her neckline, at her clavicle.

It was not designed to be tight and a choker, like an indoor collar, but it accurately represented that this person was taken and that trying to poach someone under another Dom's control or sphere of influence...

She was taken.

And I love that. But what I did not love was the intrusiveness of the DORCs. But I know it wasn't just to me; it was Jessica and every other person who was under the purview of the DORCs.

There was no known favoritism, but there was known punishment for those who did not follow or were found to be flaunting the Department of Rules and Contracts rules.

The last thing you wanted to do was embarrass that agency because they could ass fuck you so hard and for so long that it was a deterrence in and of itself. The DORCs audit was feared and dreaded.

And why not? It was like getting a proctology exam from Captain Hook (twice now).

The sheer level of psych questions reminded me of the types of questions I would ask a prospective employee during an interview many moons ago when I was in the tech world. The kind where I was trying to probe into their minds to see who they were.

Who they were is probably more appropriate, and whether I could deal with them. I can teach somebody technology; I cannot teach personality. If you're an ass douche, you're an ass douche.

I'm sure the DORCs felt similarly, and I would appreciate if they did, but the most challenging part for me was the physical testing.

If you've been following the story for some ridiculously insane reason, I have had six knee surgeries and live in tremendous pain. Jessica has been fantastic about that.

But she was astute and ensured a provision in a contract renewal several years ago that provided a bed for her of her choosing and not to be sullied by myself.

I always wanted to make sure that Jessica had everything she needed to be the best sub she could be, and I know based on the testing results that I would get, Doms got those where subs didn't.

What kind of testing are we talking about? For both of us, we had to undergo an intense psychological examination to ensure that we were mentally capable of being in a contractual relationship.

The physical one was far more interesting. Being a bit older than Jessica, I had to go through a physical wellness exam and generalized stress test on my body.

That meant treadmills, sensors, and all of that shit you would see on TV.

I always felt that it was punishment by the DORCs and good business to ensure that all parties were represented in a contract.

And therefore, under the purview of the DORCs, it did not represent the DORCs poorly. It was like covering their asses collectively. Like any governing body has done in the history of humans.

And during this round of testing, I placed in the top 75th percentile for physical endurance when it came to running on a treadmill for 30 minutes.

I just couldn't because of my knees, and I was always able to document and hand over to the DORCs all of that information so that they understood that it wasn't that I was out of shape per se, but I physically wasn't able to perform that task.

FFS, I was within the appropriate height/weight/ BMI, but having knees that were shit always cost me with the DORCs. This many years in, and I still don't understand why.

From a mental faculties perspective, I was in the top 98th percentile. Five concussions will do that to you, I can attest. I've documented that elsewhere.

More importantly, it is crucial to note that Jessica was in the top 99.7th percentile of applicants or participants in the United States.

Jessica was a phenomenal specimen of a human physically, psychologically, and emotionally, and I will say that 1 billion times over. She was extraordinary.

From the moment I saw Jessica so many years ago, and through every interaction she and I had before Christmas Eve, I knew she was astonishing.

Summary: The love to go through something, its value to me, and my disdain for dealing with tiny people whose only reason for existing is to ensure the process is incredibly challenging. While it makes it memorable and unique for all parties, it's still painful as all fuck.

This chapter, "Testing," and the upcoming "Reviews" chapter are integral to the overall story about Jessica and me and our absolute dedication and love for one another.

—————————————————————————————————

P9 - Dom

Part nine 9 of The Jessica Files, Dom. This week, we get caught up with Sir and Ma'am and learn a little more about The Department of Rules and Contracts, aka DORCs.

—-

It was a beautiful Sunday in spring, which here in Arizona runs from February till it hits 100*. That's anytime between the end of March and mid-May.

Jessica and I had gone out to a local bar one day to have a couple of drinks and watch the San Francisco Giants and the St. Louis Cardinals in a doubleheader.

We didn't go out very often, mainly because of my desire to be home. We were having a great time, but then...

I noticed this lady who seemed to be eyeballing Jessica out of the corner of my eye. And it was kind of annoying, but it wasn't harmful then.

As it got into the late afternoon, the lady decided that she would come over to our table. I wasn't sure what to expect at first. She was of average height and weight, average looking.

Once she arrived at the table, nothing seemed out of the ordinary. But then...

The lady points at Jessica and says, "I am claiming this woman as my own for contract."

I chuckled, and Jessica slowly lowered her hand underneath the table to put it on my leg because she was nervous. But Jessica knew the rules and the procedures around something like this.

"Miss, I believe you are gravely mistaken and overstepping your bounds. I recommend that you leave immediately," I forcefully stated to her.

Again, the lady proclaims, "I am claiming this woman as my own for contract." But this time, she's staring at me.

I calmly say to the lady, "You fancy yourself a Dom? Well, then, you know the rules about this, don't you?" I stared at this lady, stupid enough to try to claim shit like this.

I mean, I'm sure as fuck of the contents of that section, as it was always crucial to me. So this is going to be interesting.

The lady looked back at Jessica, trying to stare her down, but Jessica just looked down at the table, squeezing my leg more and more as this shit continued.

"You're a Dom, right? That takes precedence over gender orientation. I do not want to say this a second time... You need to turn around and walk away before I slap the ever-living shit out of you."

"You can't slap me. I'm a woman."

I quickly stood up, and everything else stopped in the bar. You could hear a pin drop. I'm guessing they know what's coming; ain't nothing good is the answer.

I told the lady, "I will give you a choice of the outcome here. I offer to buy you a shot of whatever you would like up to $100."

Damn, that's a pretty generous offer right there in my book.

"Or I'm gonna slap you so hard the DORCs will be able to identify your body by my fingerprints."

The lady freezes; I'm unsure if she was trying to calculate how hard I would hit her or what she wanted for a shot. I start a slow count in my head … one thousand and one, one thousand and two…

"I would like the Dalmore 18, please."

As I was cocking my arm back to lay waste to this thing trying to circumvent the DORCs rules, I lowered my hand to my pocket and took the one hundred dollar bill out. I always kept a hundred-dollar bill in my wallet for shit like this.

I've had that hundred dollars in my wallet for many years now. Most people apparently like being slapped.

The waitress finally comes over now that things weren't going to turn sour. "How would you like that, on the rocks, neat...?"

I turned to the waitress; I handed her the one hundred dollars I had initially noted and pulled out another hundred dollars. "I think she wanted a double, right?"

"Yes, that would be very kind of you, sir. Thank you."

"Miss, you made the right choice. But, don't ever let it happen again because some Doms are not as forgiving as I am."

The lady looked down at the table in my direction while I presume Jessica was nearly panicking.

When the waitress returned, she handed the lady a colossal drink of whatever the fuck it was. The lady looked down at her drink, swirling it around in the glass.

Finally, the lady looks up at me directly, not quite in the eyes, and says, "I'm sorry, sir. She is just so amazing."

And I replied, "I believe it's time for you to go."

Jessica and I finish our drinks, and as we are ready to go, we signal for the waitress, and she comes over again.

She says, "Thank you so much for not hitting that person. We don't want any trouble here, and we appreciate the lengths you went to prevent an incident."

I chuckled ... Incident. The bigger problem, and she and I knew it, wasn't any violence; it was the fact that the DORCs would be here really fast, and everybody would have to endure dealing with them.

"Could you bring us our bill or tell me what I owe to save time?" I asked

"Call it $40 out the door, tip included, fair?" she stated with much uncertainty. A LOT.

I handed the waitress forty dollars and said, "Thank you, have a wonderful evening."

I turn to Jessica. "Are you OK, my love?"

"Yes, Sir. But Sir, were you going to hit her?"

"Jessica, she was a Dom. Do you know what the rules are?" I paused.

"I think so, Sir," she said in a very deflated way.

"Jessica, U.S. Code 14, The Department of Rules and Contracts, Section 4, subsection 6, paragraphs 3-5, clearly note that another Dom is not allowed to poach a sub at any time, anywhere, for any reason, ever.

"Paragraphs 6 and 7 outline that I am within my rights as a Dom to take the necessary actions to protect myself and my sub, in that order, by whatever legal means necessary."

Jessica perked up. "Yes, Sir. I remember now, Sir."

Usually, Jessica waits for my hand to be out before she grabs mine, sometimes palm-in-palm, but pinky hooks are our favorite. Of course, it helps since we live in Hell. OK, fine... Phoenix, Arizona

As we left, Jessica held my hand tighter than I thought she had ever done before. I thought I knew why but would be surprised by the events.

As soon as we got outside, I ordered a RydemNow. While we stood there, Jessica turned towards me, kissed me on the cheek, and said, "Thank you, Sir."

I turned towards her, not saying anything but curious about what she was thinking.

"But, Sir, your hands belong on me and no one else!"

I smiled at Jessica.

"Sir, as per U.S. Code 14, The Department of Rules and Contracts, Section 4, subsection 6, Addendum R that was dually agreed to and signed by us...."

Wow! She knows her shit. Damn, I love this woman through and through.

"Sir, that addendum says that I am yours, and you are mine, and we shalt never touch another."

"Yes, Jessica. That's for threesomes or for either of us to fool around on the side. It's not for this."

"Oh, I see, Sir. So is that why we didn't hook up with 'eXXa' when we had the chance?"

I thought about how the spelling of her name, using the letter X instead of the letter M, made it so annoying to pronounce. And to be honest, it just irked the shit out of me.

I stared intensely at Jessica, happy with her thoughts but unsure of where she was going. I wanted to bring out more and have a happy yum-yum time.

"Jessica, I love you. I only ever, EVER, want to be with you. You and only you. Aside from the Gatos, you are the only thing that matters to me. I love you. You are mine as I am yours."

Jessica squeezed my fingers again, a little more complex, more joyous. "Thank you, Sir. I only want to be yours, for now, and always."

"Well, my love, when we get home, we'll swap your collar and ...."

I noticed her hand again rise up and gently clutch her outside collar. I know it means the world to her, as I know it fucking means the world to me. That collar is my love for her.

I often was disappointed when she did that, but I'd never said a word about it as best as I could remember.

It was something I had crafted for her, something no one else could or would ever have. It was unique, like her, and meant the world to me, like myself to her. She was just so amazing.

"Jessica, once we've swapped your collars, I will put my hands all over you!"

——

P10 - Collars

Part ten 10 of The Jessica Files, Collars. This week, we get caught up with Sir and Ma'am and learn about how their collars came to be.

—-

One evening Jessica and I were having dinner at our favorite Mom and Pop Chinese restaurant, Hello Shen Go. We went there often enough that the owners and waitstaff knew us by first and last names. It was a special place for us, so many memories there.

Jessica looked at me, smiled, and asked, "Sir, I'd like to talk with you about changing some parameters of our relationship."

My first thought was three-way. And then an old joke raced through my mind, "If I wanted to disappoint two people at the same time, I'd go to dinner with my parents." All jokes aside, I knew this was a good chat to have.

After this conversation, Jessica said she was under the impression that I would say three-way. That conversation will be saved for another day.

I turned to my left, looked at her, and said to myself;
this is a nexus point of our relationship. Am I
looking into the Eyes Of A Stranger or those of the
only woman who will wear my collar, inside and
out?

"Well, Jessica." I paused, knowing this could be a
profound statement in our relationship. "You have
my attention."

At first, Jessica smiled, but not in her typical
manner. This one was a bit different; perhaps she
was unsure how to bring up this part of the
discussion, afraid of rejection. It was strange
behavior.

Jessica popped up as if she had given herself a shot
of liquid courage. She was returning to normal-ish; I
could see how her eyes changed. Her body
language changed. I could feel it.

"Sir, you know I love you through and through. You
know I love the boys equally. You know we rarely, if
ever, spend the night without one another, knees
aside."

"Yes, Ma'am, I know. And we all do too." The boys Fluffle, Shibby, and Tibor very much like her.

"Well, Sir, do you think we could make it official? Could I officially move in with you? It's a waste of money for me to pay rent and never be there. Please, Sir?"

"Ma'am, this is the conversation I expected and have patiently awaited. You have chosen the right moment. I believe it is now that time, and this is the place.

"Jessica, I know my tone will change here, and I will explain. But please know, you are everything to me. I could only hope to symbolize that to you. I want you in every possible facet."

I paused my usual weird pause. Note to self; I do need to fix that.

"Jessica, I will happily allow you to move in with me. But I want you to wear my collar, inside and out." There, that can's now been opened, and no liquid courage was needed.

"Jessica, I realize that means we would have to deal with the Department of Rules and Contracts, the DORCs, and we will have much work to do, now and in the future.

"Dealing with the DORCs is typically very annoying, worse than the DMV, and often very brutal if you don't follow the rules. As you know, contracts are legally binding documents. That is the level of my love for you."

She stared at me, unsure what to say or think. That's a bombshell of a statement, but I held fast to what I wanted as we sat there. I just continued to gaze at her; she was so lovely.

I believe that before this conversation, every bit and every transaction that she and I had led to this point. I wanted a sub, and she was whom I wanted, and only her.

"But Sir, are you saying...?"

"Yes, Ma'am, I am saying... I want you as my sub, under contract. I want you to wear my collar, inside and out."

I continued. "I will fashion you an outside collar from things essential to me, one that I would be honored and proud for you to have and wear. One that will signify...."

Jessica interrupted. "Sir? I... I... I am speechless."

"You don't have to decide right now, Jessica, but those are my terms and what I am interested in. I know I haven't explicitly stated it before, but I have wanted it since I first saw you."

"Sir, I would be honored, and it would be a privilege to be yours. I would love to wear your collar, inside and out."

I never thought Jessica was desperate, but sometimes the rapidity of her responses to some of my demands, if you want to call them demands, has led me to feel that way. It was refreshing nonetheless.

Jessica wasn't exactly wealthy, and then again, neither was I. In many ways, I was all that she had, and more importantly, she was all that I had. And that made us wealthy as a couple.

Jessica was an incredibly unique specimen, and it wasn't until this point that I said this sentence...

"Jessica, I love you and want you to be mine."

I continued. "Jessica, I would kill all humans for you, and I will kill all humans with you. You are everything that I had ever wanted in another person.

"I waited a lifetime to meet you, I waited a lifetime to hold you, and I waited a lifetime for you to be mine." I knew that I would say this many times in the future.

I sat there, gazing at this beautiful human being. I was so lucky to have her as a part of my life, and I watched the tears roll down her cheeks. Sad but lovely at the same time.

That moment made us who we are, and that moment was extraordinary. This was the first time I would see Jessica cry, the second time being at our collar ceremony, and the third was the badness.

I put my hands out into the air and asked for her to join me. And she put her hands in mine, noticing the stillness in the absence of my usual shakiness.

"Sir? Are you OK? You aren't shaking?"

"No, Ma'am, I'm not shaking. I've never been so convinced of what I've wanted, for whom I've wanted, and why I've wanted it. Jessica, I very much do love you."

There it was, a second time around the diamond. I professed my love to her, and fuck did I mean it.

"I want you as my own, to give myself to you, so I am your own. I want the next level others hope for but are unwilling to work towards. I want all your love so I can give all of mine."

"Sir? Am I the one that you want?" And with that, how I was punished.... she broke into a cute rendition of a few verses "You're The One That I Want" from the movie Grease...

____

P11 - Reviews

Part eleven 11 of The Jessica Files. This week, we learn about performance reviews and how much they suck in the contract world, just like in the corporate world. Hooray!

—-

The idea of having to do a review of Jessica was always a painful task, just like it was for her to do mine. A Dom/sub relationship was hard to document, except it wasn't that hard.

Even though I have done many reviews in the past, my absolute love for her makes it more of a challenge every review cycle. She was extraordinary; I've had to deal with that from outside interests.

As per the Department of Rules and Contracts, or DORCs, every Dom and sub was required to file a yearly evaluation of our goals and accomplishments, akin to having yet another corporate job.

If you have ever dealt with any government entity, you know something like a performance review is akin to bamboo shoots under your fingernails. Fucking brutal.

The thing is, all of this went on our permanent record. The data that the DORCs compiled was admissible in court. It was legally binding documentation.

Jessica and I were always honest and never really sucked up to one another during the performance reviews.

Good lord, you used the wrong phrase. I've seen people cut down at the knees (no pun) over shit like that. You had to maintain their language and diction. We're talking about DORCs here.

I always tried to give Jessica positive feedback and constructive criticism above and beyond the corrective actions from the requirements. It always was a nightmare for me. I was so in love with Jessica.

Jessica was a fantastic specimen of a human and someone I loved beyond this realm without a doubt. She was absolute, like Time itself, and not just in her beauty but in her humanity.

If I were one of those crazy people who wanted to start a new version of the human race in an untainted way, her essence would be one of the most important that I could cultivate.

Jessica was exceptional. She was the epitome of excellence, and I loved her as no man had ever loved anybody before. She was the best of the best, of the best.

But there was a downside to Jessica. While she was an extraordinary sub, there were several things that I continued to feel that she could do better, and I tried to coach her, but it didn't always work.

There were 3 to 5 bullet points that I was to give as an accurate representation of the relationship, as per the DORCs. Those fucking DORCs are always up in people's shit.

I swear to Zeus that those fucks only did it to mess around with people. I mean, is that not what government is for?

While I didn't particularly appreciate having to do these reviews, I always loved getting Jessica's feedback, wherein she was in a safe environment.

There was no recourse to how she felt and acted; she could provide feedback safely and securely. You have no idea how important that was to me.

I could probably discipline her more, and I have noted such several times with my paperwork. I loved that facet of the contract. 1,000% loved that facet.

I could hear what she was saying outside of our contract, even if it fell under the purview of a government organization. It gave her an all-important voice, a voice to be heard.

And I was always listening.

Jessica and I knew that this was required by the Department of Rules and Contracts. If you are going to live a contract life, you must deal with the consequences.

Those consequences included dealing with legalese, creating documentation about your sub or Dom, and filing with the DORCs weekly. What a pain in the ass!

I always did my best to honestly and accurately represent how I felt towards the relationship and all of the critical markers regarding how the DORCs graded things.

I'll say it once, if not a million times, that Jessica was the one, and she is the only one who has worn my collar. She is everything I had ever wanted a companion, furniture, friend, lover, everything.

And I wrote that to the DORCs in my review many times over.

I know that I could not live my life without Jessica, and she knew that well but never did utilize that as an exploit in our relationship.

I believe that we both knew from the second we saw one another.

I asked Jessica about the reviews one morning to ensure she did her part.

"Yes, Sir, I feel that my reviews are complete."

"That's wonderful, Ma'am. I don't need to know anything other than that you had accomplished the required task.

"And you know how that would make me look, regardless of the content of the review, but if you didn't do your job, where would we be?"

Jessica looked at me and smiled. It was a kind smile that broke me as a human. As a kind smile on Christmas Eve.

With a slight head nod, I smiled and suggested that Jessica should come to me. It was more of a call for a kiss than anything else.

She came to me, and I pulled her in close to hold her, and she was against me like said Christmas Eve.

I whispered into her ear, "I love you, Jessica. There will be no other. You are mine as I am yours. Forever."

I hate to use the term pair-bonded, but I think we were many years ago, which shows in the relationship. It shows in everything we do as a couple. I just wanted my Jessica.

And whenever I would say something like that or have those feelings, I am reminded of the realities where there was no Jessica. The ones where she walked away, and I did not stop her.

All the pain and disappointment awakened us in a sadness that could not be understood unless seen from our wonderful life together.

While we don't always do the right things per se, there are times when we make decisions that are based on her humanity and not on the rules, not on the language of the contract.

But we are not harming one another with any malicious intent.

We love the fuck out of each other, and I didn't need a collar on her to prove it. I loved having a collar on her because it proved how much she meant to me.

And I know Jessica loved me because she lived the life of a sub, my sub, and performed her role. She loved me because she wanted this lifestyle as millions of others did.

"Jessica, do you love me? Do you love me with all of your being? Would you cut your hand off for me? Would you do that right now, upon my request?"

Jessica replied in her typical instantaneous manner, "Sir, I will cut my hand off for you, Sir. Tell me which one; I will do so, Sir."

And then the hesitation that I'd come to both expect and love from my Jessica. "But Sir, it would make my servitude to you much more difficult, and I'm afraid the DORCs would penalize us!"

And she was right, and they would be a problem to us. She was astute, such an intelligent human. My human.

And it was things like this that I would use to capture and articulate my feelings towards Jessica and how she performed as my sub in my yearly reviews.

"Jessica, I love you too much to do something like that, let alone ask you to. Surely, it would make many things in our life more difficult."

"Like what, Sir?"

I looked at Jessica, at first frowning, but that slowly, with much pace, grew into a giggle, knowing what I was going to say was outlandish and silly, classic this guy.

"Jessica, don't forget to cup the balls." Such a brilliant reference to SuperTroopers, a favorite of ours.

____

P12 - First Last Always

Part twelve 12 of The Jessica Files, FLA. This week, we get caught up with Sir and Ma'am and why they are the First Last Always with one another.

—-

▌▌First Last Always" is a trio of ideas based on a song from The Sisters Of Mercy called "First and Last and Always." This chapter is about how this concept has strengthened Jessica and me.

- The first person I want to see or talk to in the morning. Mine!
- The last person I want to see or speak to at night. Mine!
- And the person always on my mind and in my dreams. Mine!

I remember the first time I realized this statement would have come true for me a couple of days after Christmas night.

The events that transpired were also significant catalysts to what Jessica and I are. It's genuinely fantabulous.

Jessica was unbelievable, and it was undeniable the power that she projected when she was with me.

She was much timider when she was by herself, but it was twice as much power when she had me by her side. That might not make much sense, but Jessica was energetic yet sensitive to her energy.

And I was as well, which meant that it was far more intense for the two of us than while we were apart versus when we were together. It was powerful and enticing.

The energy we had together was fantastic, and it was a great human connection between us; I think we both knew that on Christmas Eve so many years ago.

It was cemented Christmas Night and the following morning. We were both still there. We wanted to be there. That was the beginning.

It wasn't, but a few nights after that Christmas Night date, no, we would spend the vast majority of the many years that brings us to the present that we did not spend our night together.

Falling asleep with one another in blissful happiness, two souls intertwining, was how we wanted to spend the last moments before Ambien won that battle.

Jessica had this feel to her, even as far back as the Christmas Eve hug.

I don't know how anybody she had ever been around or with did not pick it up, but there was an energy there that was kinetic, at least for me, from the moment we touched.

Very often, when we touched, it was like scuffing your feet while wearing socks on the carpet in the winter and zapping somebody you live with or around you. It was like a Christmas thing.

It was such a great feeling to have that touch with somebody. But I can still feel the zap in her kiss, even if we have a home that is entirely vinyl tile.

The tile was to prevent that type of shit from happening, even by accident. I always knew she got a rise out of it. So I paid for the flooring upgrade.

After we touched, I never wanted to be without Jessica because I felt something so weird and unique that I knew before she even professed her love for me on Christmas night.

I knew that she was the one. The one. I am not going to do it again.

At least in this reality, we are thrilled and willing to push ourselves to incredible lengths to be the people who best exemplify this lifestyle and why there was so much love there.

Jessica is brilliant and is the financial mastermind in our family. She is an economic whiz and ensured that we always had a fair balance of bills paid, money saved, and fun things to be done.

She worked part-time because she could get away for 25 hours a week, but she got to do something that she enjoyed doing. And it gave me the time I needed to do my job, writing about things of interest, which I found very interesting.

The money she made there was hers, always hers. Not hers like our money, but hers. I demanded that it be put into the contract. Where would we be if we did shit we didn't like when working?

That brings me to Tuesdays because Tuesdays are when she works in the afternoons into the evenings and the day I looked forward to immensely.

Tuesday's meant a ceremonial color exchange and the spankings for leaving the house schtick. Not complaining is this Dom. Ecstatic for it is this Dom.

Jessica being out of the house for a while was incredibly beneficial. It gave me a way to give her an out where she could leave and be that Jessica for a little while.

I believe that that was imperative to our relationship and most successful relationships would be very well aligned with that statement.

You have to have a little bit of "you" time even if your time is going to work and getting paid for it.

But Jessica being out throughout the day typically leads to me thinking about her, and there's very little in this world that I enjoy more than thinking about Jessica.

However, when she got home, that was the most exciting part of the day, perhaps the week. Far and above, and beyond whatever I was thinking about when Jessica got home.

What happened next was based on our energy together as a couple. It was the basis of whether or not I would be sitting on a floor cushion applying an ice pack to her ass.

I've mentioned a time before; I looked forward to our collar exchange on Tuesdays.

I would have Jessica under her indoor collar for almost two days because she didn't return to work until Thursday.

That meant she had to wear her indoor collar that entire time and I loved that. I loved her indoor collar for what it symbolized when she wore it. It meant a lot to me, Dom-wise.

I also knew her outdoor collar meant infinitely more to me. Her outdoor collar was something that I constructed for her out of things from my past. It was my gift to her.

I didn't go to Jared for some infinity necklace or crap. I made this for her because I love her, and she means much to me. She's that special.

I'll probably note this a lot, Jessica was absolute, like time, except for those realities where she and I weren't together. Those were saddening.

There was a ritual for bedtime that I don't believe I've mentioned, something above and beyond Big/little spoon.

This was wherein if I was upset with her and did not want to discipline her physically, she would be commanded to sit on the floor by my side of the bed.

That's punishment, part one.

She would have to sit there until I'd indicated she could join me or until she could discern from the snoring or the shuddering of my body in pain that she could get into bed.

That's punishment, part two.

And where would we be without the concern of a rule violation with the DORCs?

And that would be punishment, part three.

Yes, it violated that provision in the contract, but it was rarely prosecuted. First time saying that too. Yes, court prosecution was the DORCs' way of saying "Thank You."

People didn't want to mess with the DORCs because they had unlimited money if they sued you. You had not-unlimited money. *doing the math here*

As much as I'd like to think otherwise, the DORCs were my first and last and always. I worried a lot due to their known wrath. I already supposed they didn't care for me based on testing stuff.

I was always concerned in any of my interactions with the DORCs. They always felt like the Gestapo, but I knew they had to be strict in order to protect this lifestyle.

I know that in this lifetime, I get my Jessica. The first person I wanted to speak to in the morning. And the first person I see in the morning.

The person I want to be, my little spoon. The last person I want to talk to before bed.

And Jessica was always on my mind. So many years ago, she was always on my mind, presenting how true love can manifest.

————————————————————————————————————

P13 – Friday Night

Part thirteen 13 of The Jessica Files. This week, we learn about realities in life and how it has affected Sir and Ma'am, and how there could be and not be a contract life.

—-

There were very few nights in which Jessica and I did not spend the night together from Christmas night to this day, however many years it is now.

We loved falling asleep together, connecting, and feeling wanted and respected. It was a fantastic feeling, and it was something that Jessica and I held onto dearly.

As if it was something missing in our lives.

I'm going to describe to you or relate a particular Friday night I did and didn't have my Jessica and what it was like.

I'm sure it would be worse now not to have my Jessica. To not have my love and my one. The one. I will not be doing it again.

I don't specifically recall the reasoning as to why we were apart that night, but I presume it was a family-related thing. I'd have to ask her, and that's not the point.

If you would think, being alone for the night, a Friday night was like some party time and all kinds of chicanery.

It underscored the level for which this woman was so important to me and how she fit into my life and made it whole.

I motioned Jessica to come over, as I would whenever I wanted a kiss. As she stood before me, nearly nose to nose, our smiles reflected our love for one another. She was very special to me, and I let my kiss show her how I felt and loved her.

After such a sweet and loving kiss, I opened up a new bottle of red wine, filled up her glass, and then my own.

As I set the bottle down, some thoughts raced through my mind. I believed there were infinite realities in which I did this by myself on a Friday night. I don't have Jessica with me, and my life is incomplete.

I've seen the carnage of a life without her. I've seen it over and over and over. And I will detail that in another chapter.

I lifted my glass and toasted Jessica; with a slight clank, I said, Here's to the eve of the day which will never come; here is to retreat to ease the pain." From the Antidote by Moonspell.

That was always my toast of choice for the last 15 years. There is so much to signify in the quote that it would be hard for me to spend excessive time dissecting it.

I will note that it means I don't ever want to be without her because I will have to be in immense pain to traverse that. And I do not believe I would even try.

Tonight, she wasn't here, and I didn't have my Jessica. And I would forget that from time to time as I would turn and she wasn't there.

I would have a conversation with her, and she wasn't there. I knew that I felt so incredibly lost; no words.

And we had sips of our wine; I looked at Jessica, and I just looked at her. I looked at this beautiful and unique, fantastical human whom I loved like there was no tomorrow.

I often watch Jessica move; the fluidity of her movements was just...

It was amazing to be so in love with somebody for so long, so many years, even still, and think of the person I was with as the most incredible fucking person on the planet.

That was contract life.

Because I couldn't be with Jessica in our world without that, and while it brought us the stability and security in a relationship we both craved, she did so much for me.

It just did so much for the two of us. I always say I can't speak for her, but I always know because she was my sub.

We often spent so much time staring into one another's eyes without having a conversation, just sitting there, staring.

It was beyond surreal, but I always knew how loving it was for us to do that. She was so... so Jessica.

My point here is that there is a duality in our lives; some things happen, and others don't.

We don't always get what we want, and regardless of what we wish for, if we were to get it, it would be excruciating, and we could not handle it. And that is why wishes are incredibly rarely granted.

But this night, I could always reach out to her and have a conversation with and without her being here at home. They were paramount to our overall success.

But of all the things between us, Jessica had access to the only two essential things to me.

One, the boys, and two, my heart. In that order. The boys, Shibby and Tibor.

I always knew that the only thing she could harm me with was her love, but I never felt like it was an external threat to me, my existence, and, subsequently, to the boys' well-being.

Jessica was adorable in this regard, where she enjoyed proving herself to me, but that was the life of a sub, and goddamn, she was good at it.

I never had a reason to doubt her, but it was in the standard DORCs contract that a level of communication is necessary when two parties are apart.

And we both signed that line, and we worked our asses off to ensure that the other party was in the loop and know, that there was no doubt.

I would never fucking accept any level of doubt from her. And I would never give it to her in some reciprocal hell.

I love my Jessica, and I turned to give her a clank, and she was both there and not at the same time.

I would not ask somebody to do something in my life; in my work, I would never ask somebody to do something I was unwilling to do. And I felt the same way towards Jessica and the contract.

I would not ask her to tell me where she was if I was unwilling to do the same when I was not with her. Thankfully I rarely left the house.

Even when I did, I always ensured that I let Jessica know at every stop and turn because I expected the same in return.

And that's what contracts are all about. You agree with another person and the DORCs and are bound to uphold the said agreement. I don't think that's a complex statement to understand.

I wouldn't say I liked these nights; I can recall around five in total, but that was five too many for me. I always wanted my Jessica because I saw the other side.

I don't mean to harp on the fact, but there is a plain truth: I did not get my Jessica in some realities. What I got was heartbreak and disappointment, and so did she.

She is all I have ever wanted, and I have had her in my hand and watched it go to sand that I could not catch. I don't mean to be sad.

On a Friday night, I wish she was here; we not only drank copious amounts of wine, but we also would cook dinner together.

This was more me attempting to cook than her because she was a far better cook than I could ever hope to be. Far, far, far better.

But Friday night was my night to be dull and shine.

We made pork chops with carrots, mini potatoes, and red onions in the oven this Friday night. It was a delicious treat because I would season everything with Special Shit.

Yeah, I love Special Shit. It is the bomb.

Once we had gotten everything together and the oven up to temp, everything was set, and we had 22 minutes on the clock until we needed to pull stuff out.

I looked at Jessica and said, "Ma'am, fancy yourself a quickie?"

Jessica's eyes lit up, and I may not have finished that sentence before she was in front of me; she grabbed my hand, making our way out of the kitchen.

These things weren't about me; they were all about Jessica. 100% just Jessica. I can't say that enough; whenever I said "fancy a quickie," it was not about this guy.

It made me feel so complete as a human to have that particular type of relationship and time together that it wasn't about me.

After 22 minutes, we were back in the kitchen, cleaned up, ready to finish cooking dinner, and sat down for another lovely meal together.

And so we did. I brought Jessica a well-crafted plate of what we had just cooked, and after setting it down in front of her, I raised my head to gaze at Jessica.

While neither of us smoked cigarettes, I knew that look I saw on Jessica's face; she REALLY wanted one.

____

P14 - The Rules

Part fourteen 14, of The Jessica Files. This week, we get caught up on the Rules. This is life; this is what they live. And they love it.

—-

Jessica and I live in a world that The Department of Rules and Contracts controls, but it is not required to be under their purview.

Most people who seek entry into this lifestyle are denied based on the testing criteria put forth by the DORCs. Many requirements are placed upon applicants.

The essential part of living this lifestyle is the consequences of violating the rules and even bigger ones for lying about them.

The DORCs are not very forgiving and have been known to punish the shit out of people for violating their contracts with the DORCs, not just with their partners. Lots of lawsuits there too.

By punished, I mean that the DORCs would first perform a standard audit of both parties, requiring supporting documentation for any activities during that contract's life.

The DORCs would drag people through the court system and sue them for breach of contract if the audit was not to their liking. And it never was. You could never win.

It is ugly, painful, and completely unnecessary.

The best and saddest part is that the DORCs won nearly all cases because the contract was very explicit about the rules and regulations, roles, and expectations.

If you violated them, you'd be subpoenaed and then dragged through the court system, which was always incredibly painful, especially in a smaller community like that under the DORCs.

The contracts had many ins and outs, but the most important thing when dealing with the DORCs was being absolutely transparent and infinitely honest.

There was no reason to get into trouble unless you were a troublemaker. And some were, and you would hear about them, but their time would come.

Jessica and I took our relationship exceptionally seriously and did everything we could to follow the rules.

Given that we had to file weekly status reports with the DORCs, knowing that we would get audited if things were out of sorts, we lived by the contract.

And the vast majority of people under contract did so as well. It was paramount. As I mentioned before, you could never win.

You could not succeed in this lifestyle if you didn't follow the rules set forth by the DORCs, let alone follow the rules set aside for you and your partner.

There are many different setups, but it always came down to two people who identified however they wanted; the DORCs didn't give a shit about that, a Dom and sub (or D/s).

We knew of subsections of this where the two people in the contract would "switch" from Dom and sub as they saw fit. And the DORCs didn't care.

They just wanted everyone to follow the same set of rules. And that even was true for people who contracted as Dom/slave. I understood that, but I didn't get it.

One of the contractual agreements between two parties is made between a third party, the DORCs. The D/s were bound to one another, but both were bound to the DORCs.

You didn't have to uphold yourself to your partner, but you sure as shit best to the DORCs if you wanted to succeed.

That's where testing comes into play, reviews come into play, and something I've mentioned briefly in the past, but the weekly reports to the DORCs.

In our day and time, we have the opportunity of submitting the weekly status reports to the DORCs online via their secure system.

From what I understand back in the day, it was handwritten and sent to the DORCs via the mail or dropped off at approved drop boxes.

That would be incredibly inconvenient as we look at it in our day and age.

Nonetheless, if you did not file your weekly status report by Sunday night, you would hear about it bright and early Monday morning from the DORCs.

And while it was unpleasant, there were times when you would communicate with them that a specific event was going on beforehand. Beforehand.

Let me say that a third time BEFOREHAND. Informing the DORCs after you failed to execute your contractual obligations was on you, and man, that was all over you.

Like a ton of bricks made of shit, covered in shit. As I stated earlier, it is essential to understand that you are willfully entering a contract with a government agency.

The government agency's most important directive is to protect the government agency. I kid you not.

Just like ANY and EVERY other government agency.

The weekly status report wasn't as bad as I feel I'm making it, but it was awful because of the details. And many details were required.

As in other writings, you must know the events that have transpired. Like the badness, I had to detail all of my actions to bring Jessica into compliance again.

I had to detail everything required to bring her into compliance against my will, but that is what was contractually agreed upon. It still hurts me knowing it had gone that far.

And by agreed-upon, I mean you have to have legal representation and go through line by line of the contract that was at least 75 pages at a 6pt font.

Before you get to the personalized entries into the agreement, like a new bed for Jessica in the guest room that I won't sully.

The number of additional entries into a contract could be vast and extensive or none, and it came down to the individuals submitting the contract.

184

And as I noted in the past, there were times when we line-item-approved things because we knew how important they were, and we also had to ensure that those things were merged forward.

We had to ensure all of that was in the next contract because every time your contract came up for renewal, you got a standard document to which you had to add all of your previous agreements.

It was always exciting to note how meticulous the DORCs were when reviewing a contract with an addendum, like the bed. Think painful.

They went through everything. And that is why you have legal representation for yourself, as did your partner. It was all legal wrangling and bullshit.

But that is what Jessica and I wanted, we wanted the safety and security of contract life, and we understood we would have to deal with the DORCs and their orders.

I love my Jessica, and she loves her Sir. We've been doing this for many years, successfully, lovingly, happily, under many contracts, following the rules.

____

P15 - Handoff

Part fifteen 15 of The Jessica Files. This week, we learn
about handoffs, their reality, and how they affect Sir
and Ma'am in a contract life.

—-

Oh, how Tuesday nights are so exciting in
this household. I've written about them in
the past and how Jessica and I had to
follow etiquette with the contract.

There is so much in our relationship, in any
contract relationship, and a large swath of a
contract is repetition. You repeat the same tasks
over and over and over, and with much love.

The contract gave Jessica and me the structure we
needed to succeed in a relationship. We had
unknowingly craved it for so many years until our
orbits gravitated.

When Jessica worked on Tuesdays, I longed for the
events always to transpire. A unique set of rules for
this evening, as dually agreed to with the DORCs.

"Sir, I'm home!" she'd proclaimed as if I weren't waiting for her in the kitchen, like a kid on Christmas morning. It was always a boost on top of love. It was something extraordinary.

I always tried to be in my place when I heard the garage go. Jessica would come in, set her stuff down, and come into the kitchen to address me.

When she would come into the kitchen, I could always see that thing we see in someone we love, that we long to be with. Like on Christmas Eve, on Christmas Night.

"Sir? Shall I...?"

"Jessica, you shalt."

She stood just in front of me and turned away from me, bowing her head so slightly with her hair pulled up. It was like this every time.

I gently removed her outdoor collar, guiding it around and off of her and into my hands for me to keep safe until she was to leave the house again with my permission.

She said, "Sir, would you put my inside collar on me, please?" And so I did—Ahh, contracts, how they do things for all parties involved. It's the DORCs, you know.

I reached around her neck and chest and set Jessica's inside collar upon her. I knew she preferred her outdoor collar, given that I made it for her because I loved the fuck out of her.

I gave the woman I loved something of and from me through and through. That was as priceless as the gift, time and again, that we all have experienced.

Many thanks to the contract with the DORCs. What will they scheme up next?

I so loved the repetition of the contract and contract life. We knew what we should say and do, as if in a play.

Jessica asked, "Sir, may I?"

I replied, "You may."

She slid down her pants; oh boy, she looked fantastic. I could see that the changes in her regimen had paid off. I'm so glad I made that adjustment.

Her pants were now down at her ankles; Jessica fixed back on my eyes as she stood before me. It wasn't a showdown; she was waiting on my command.

I smirked and said, "Assume the position, Ma'am." And with that command, Jessica was on all fours with her pants down around her ankles while resting on the anti-fatigue pad.

"Sir, I was bad today. I left the house without you, and I accept the punishment that comes with it."

We both damn well knew she left the house for her job, but it's a ritual we live by and many others in the contract world. Also, it's in the contract.

I replied, "How many times were we bad, Ma'am?"

190

Jessica softly replied, as she always did, with some arbitrary number of spanks she could take without whimpering, even if Jessica knew she'd had difficulty sitting later.

I used to think of her as a trooper, but as the years passed, I knew she was a masochist, which is why we were together. Not just on contract but because of absolute love.

Jessica replied, "2, Sir."

"Ok, three it is."

There was a pause; I knew this pause. It's either goodness or badness, and I've seen things spiral out of hand here.

"Sir, I did not intend to deceive you with how many spanks I deserve."

Another lagging pause.

"Sir, you know I love you through and through. Sir, please give my ass a proper pounding. Please, Sir?"

I was uncertain if she was having fun with her wording or if that was what she wanted. So I had to ask...

"Jessica... are you asking me to pound your ass?" I giggled.

"Yes, Sir. Please."

"Jessica, I hate to ask this again, but do you want me to pound your ass?"

"Yes, Sir, I'm sorry if I stuttered, Sir. But, Sir, my ass needs you to lay into it."

My giggling got a bit louder. I'm still not sure if she's fucking with me or isn't being attentive to her words. She's not been known to do either of those things since we were in contract.

"Ok, Jessica, I'm going to really lay into your ass; I will make you feel me." At this point, my giggles were nearly out of control.

I fixed that with one hell of a spank. My hand stung for a few minutes from how hard I slapped Jessica's ass. Ask me to pound your ass; guess what happens?

"All right, Jessica. I am going to destroy your ass. You will not be able to sit right for a week. You will not be able to shit right for a week. Let me reiterate; I am going to destroy your ass."

"Sir, yes, please, Sir. Harder, like you really mean it. Please, Sir, wreck my ass. I want you to fuck my shit up!"

And suddenly, my mood and feelings changed. Rapidly. I went from being excited and turned on to what I was feeling now, nauseated and uncomfortable. Not exactly normal.

This put me at odds with myself. I did not want to escalate this, nor did I want to perform the third spank. I wanted my Jessica, the only woman to have worn my collar, inside and out.

"Jessica, please stand up."

There's the please word, again. Wow.

And in an instant, there she was. Pants down around her ankles, smiling at me as if nothing had happened. I was perplexed; something strange was afoot at the Circle K.

"Jessica, please take your shirt and bra off. Then, pull your underwear down to your ankles with your pants. Now."

"Sir, yes, Sir."

And with that, she was naked aside from her pants and underwear around her ankles.

I stood there, never bothering to take in the view of this most excellent and gorgeous specimen of a human. I just looked at Jessica's eyes, her face. I was so in love; it was painful.

I wanted to be the good cop and the bad cop simultaneously. I wanted to show and prove my love to her and not have to do more paperwork with the DORCs. It was bad enough already.

"Jessica, I want you off the record, NOW," I proclaimed with much force.

"Yes, Punis, what is the matter?"

"I love you, Jessica; there will never be any doubt over that; it's a fact. It is beyond through and through. I love you with every bit of my existence, past, present, future."

I took a deep breath, knowing what I would say could have ramifications on our relationship for the entirety of our contract and any further if we were to have any.

"Jessica, I cannot hurt you any further tonight, not like this. I love you too much to beat you physically. It is against what I believe in my core; my love for you is greater than anything else."

I paused to catch my breath from that statement; this is hard to put together.

"Jessica, I just whipped you at 100% with my belt. You did not move; you did not make any sounds. I am afraid I will push things too far and love you too much."

Jessica just stood there, naked, listening and not interjecting, even though we were off the record. That's a unique and hidden provision in the contract we exploit from time to time.

I continued, "I accept the punishment I must face so I do not hurt our love. I do not wish to hurt you, Jessica. I just..."

I went silent, lost in what I was saying but awash with many feelings proving to be much more painful as the conversation continued.

"I cannot spank you further tonight, Jessica. I am afraid of myself right now; I do not want to hurt you. I feel like I will be excessive, and I...."

I trailed off again while thinking about disciplining her and the other side, the one where she wasn't there. I know, I know. I think about that a lot, but I've seen it.

"But Punis, that was our negotiated agreement. You said three, and I am obliged to do that. I will not argue with you or file this with the DORCs. That would be unnecessary."

I stood there, nearly nose to nose with my love of all loves, discussing my punishing her ass with her. It's ludicrous.

"But Sir, you are all I will ever want, all I will ever need. You, Punis Russi, are everything I could have ever dreamed of in a mate. Before the contract and now. You are spectacular."

"Jessica..." And I started to feel like I was going to cry. I love this woman so incredibly much, so intensely as to subject myself to all the pain that comes with contract life.

"I love you, Jessica. From my first breath until now, and for every breath I will yet take in my life.

"Jessica, we are still off the record. I want you to know that I love you; you know this to be true. But I have to ask this... Do you want the third strike?"

Without hesitation, Jessica grabbed my hands, looked me in the eyes, and replied, "Punis, I'd rather we go into the bedroom and take my pounding that way."

Jessica paused, eyes probing mine like a million times in the past and to come. I never could figure out what she was thinking during these sessions; I just knew how I felt.

"Punis, I would like to go back on the record, please."

I nodded.

"Sir, why don't we go to the bedroom, and I can take my pounding there as you see fit?"

I smiled. God damn, she was astonishing.

"But, Sir, can I take off my pants before going to the bedroom? It would be rather awkward to shuffle in such a manner."

I smiled again at Jessica and nodded. She leaned over to me and gave me a sweet and tender kiss. She removed her pants and underwear, smiled at me while she turned, and walked away.

As I watched this most beautiful human walk away
from me towards the bedroom, that dark feeling
that I had watched her walk away before, on
Christmas Eve Day, swarmed over me.

I knew that I wanted my little spoon right now; I just
wanted to be able to hold my Jessica.

But first, I would have to give her an ass pounding
in the bedroom, something I always loved before I
got the chance to hold my Jessica.

————————————————————————————————————

P16 - The Alice Side

Part sixteen 16 of the Alice Files. This week, we learn more about The Alice Side and what that means to Punis in a world without his Alice.

—-

I recall thinking about this gal I was interested in; I didn't know her name, but when I would gush about her, my friends knew her as STNR. For this sake, I will refer to her as "Alice."

Alice worked at a grocery store I frequented. I was shopping that day to get supplies to make meatballs and sauce; this gal, Alice, was stocking a refrigerated case and had turned around to get more of whatever she was restocking.

Alice saw me from the corner of her eye and made a beeline to me. I wasn't expecting anything, to be honest, but the next five minutes changed both our lives.

As she got closer, her smile got seemingly wider. And her eyes, well fuck, I don't know if I can express how I felt when I looked into her eyes.

What happened next was utterly unexpected.

Alice's arms started to reach out to me. I didn't
know what the fuck was happening. I felt like a
panic attack was coming on, not like that was
anything new.

And then Alice hugged me. I couldn't believe what
was going on; this was unimaginable. Never in my
life would I have seen this one coming. So surreal.

We did that explorative dance with our eyes,
darting from one focus point to another. After the
hug, we stood in front of each other, not three feet
(arm's length) apart.

Alice was taller than any other woman (if I recall
correctly) I had been with. I had tended to date tiny
gals. Five-foot-one inch, 100lbs with a towel. That
was my wheelhouse.

Alice was five feet nine and one half inches tall, and
I stood a mere five foot eleven inches. Of course,
I'm much more accustomed to a different frame.
But that did not matter; I was still stunned by the
events.

We were nearly at eye level, looking at one another as we had a conversation. The type of conversation you typically both remember and forget simultaneously.

It was glorious. We discussed our holiday plans, whom we had (in general) in our lives, and the sadness we both held onto at the time. Family. Well, parents.

I won't divulge it here, but we both have our own shit, just like everyone else. Alice made me believe she was trying to own it, and as we all know, I own my own shit.

That meandered the discussion into our holiday plans. I didn't have any, for I was on call for some stupid fucking reason. But then again, those clowns...

Alice told me that she didn't have any plans. I took note of that. You don't tell someone that if not for a reason. But I've long believed that you don't hit on someone at their workplace.

It was bad form.

Just as the conversation was getting to be rather interesting, the PA came on asking for all associates to go to the service desk. In some lives, I stopped her and introduced myself; in others...

And with that, she turned to walk away. Then, having taken a step or two, she paused and turned around, catching me staring at her ass. I smiled.

I recall wondering if that was the end, like it had been with my friend "Andrea" from Florida. That "ass walking away type of moment," if you will. Hmm, I wonder if that'll catch on.

Once I had come back to earth, seemingly hours later, but in reality, a few moments, I texted a friend of mine who was familiar with the Sapphire Chronicles.

She was enthusiastic for me but hesitant to be all in pending that following conversation. I agreed, but I felt I knew what would come to pass.

I told her, "Dana, this is it. For real. This is a win of epic proportions. With just a hug, I am hooked on a human I have respectfully admired from a safe distance."

Dana knew the quality of the person I was (and am), and she knew I wasn't about changing the integrity that I value so highly on something so dumb as a piece of ass.

Dana asked me. "So, did you get her name? Is it something besides Alice? Lol... But seriously, did you get her number?"

Still in a haze, riding my emotions ten miles high, I said, "No. I didn't want to do that while she was at work. What do you think about me coming back the day after Christmas? I will ask Alice."

———————————————————————————————————

"It's Tuesday night, Tohru; you know what that means! Yup, it's a Tohru Tuesday!"

I was in the kitchen with Tohru that evening. He was still small and fluffy, yet, he was still a colossal asshole, as has been my experience with Ragdolls. More likely, he was just one of my whole family.

I recall talking with Tohru as he chased a ball around the kitchen, often leaving it next to me and patiently waiting for me to pick it up and throw it.

He was a fetch kitty, just like my previous excellent life companion Ragdoll, whom I lost when he was 16. He had a stellar life and received all the possible love that a cat that wasn't a Maine Coon could hope for.

I had thrown Tohru's ball across the kitchen, perhaps some 15 ft from myself, and he charged off to retrieve it. It was adorable; he's something else.

And then... my phone started to blow up from monitoring at work. Another mystery to putting someone new on-call during Christmas was beyond dumb.

But pay me a ton of money at that time, and like any person, I'd swap memory out of desktop computers with no ill will. Try to hire me like that, and you can suck my balls.

And with that, I poured myself another Cromulent Vodka/Zevia, just how I liked it. Straight to the brim, slurp it to move it. So many years on now, I still pour them like that.

I turned to Tohru, smiled at him, and toasted him the toast I always use… "Here is to the eve of the day which will never come; here is to retreat to ease the pain."

I reached down, got his toy, tossed it across the room, and slowly stood up, groaning about my knees. The pain from my shit-ass knees reminds me of the limitations I have. FUCK!

I was very excited to see Alice in two days, I would properly introduce myself and get her name, finally, so I wouldn't have to keep referring to her as Alice.

But it was time to make meatballs and sauce.

——

It was Thursday morning, bright and early. Even though I was off today, I got up at 5 AM. Hard habit to break during the week. I had so much to do, so much on my mind.

And one of those things on my mind was Alice. I was so excited to go to the store and introduce myself. I didn't know what time to go, that being a rather sizable problem.

I asked Dana, and she said, "1 PM should be a reasonable time for the day after Christmas. Just a guess."

So, around 1 PM that day, I went to the store to introduce myself to her and get some supplies. Mainly Zevia because I did hit the vodka hard on Christmas Day.

I meandered about the store, shopping but all the while looking around for Alice. But I didn't see her, and I saw pretty much everyone else that was familiar.

As I was finishing up, but before checking out, I went over to one of the managers there and asked her:

"I wanted to thank a gal who helped me on Tuesday with some stuff, but I don't know her name. She's tall, brown hair, tattoos nowhere near as good as mine...."

I was not prepared for her response. "She's no longer with us."

I was shocked and devastated. How? What? What the fuck?!? How could this happen? How could this be? Is she fucking with me? Why does this shit happen to me?

"Oh. I'm sorry." I walked to one of the checkout lanes while trying to wrap my head around this dramatic turn of events. Yet another shit show earth event that splattered on this guy.

I got into my car and readied to call Dana to tell her what had happened. I started to cry as I sat there. How had I fucked up so much to miss a chance like this?

I thought this was a chance, but who knows... she could have been a bible thumper, a meth head, or anything aside from my own.

I had lost a chance, but the only lesson I learned was that I didn't get the opportunity to lose; that was already determined for me. You could never win, you see now?

——

P17 - Tear

Part seventeen 17 of The Jessica Files, Tear. This week, we get caught up with Sir and Ma'am and this reality that grounds them to one another.

—-

One evening, I was in the kitchen making Jessica and myself a lovely Cromulent Vodka/Zevia (caffeine-free Ginger Ale) with a splash of lime (to ward off scurvy), all the way to the brim like I liked to make them.

"Jessica, my love, I have something for ya!"

"Yes, Sir, be right there."

I stood in the kitchen on my favorite anti-fatigue pad, having set our drinks on the kitchen island. I closed my eyes, thinking about Jessica and seeing her walking into the room.

And when she did, I lost my brain...thought...thing... stuff. WTF just happened?

"Jessica?" I was stunned and blown away, but just because... well...

"Sir, are you OK, Sir? Is there something I can do for you, Sir? Do we need to get medical attention, Sir?"

"Jessica, I'm OK. I... I... I can't put my words together. I'm OK, but by Zeus, you are, by far, the most beautiful human on this planet. You are breathtaking."

"Sir, is it because of this outfit? You did get it for me a long while ago. I'm sorry, Sir, I wasn't prepared to wear it yet, Sir."

That meant it was about the regimen I had put her on and how she'd taken hold of it, driving herself to please me. And why wouldn't she? She knew I was always doing the same.

But she constantly pushed herself like that, never truly realizing how much I loved her. From myself, my core, I loved this woman through and through, like none other.

I just stared at her; I was looking at something I'd kill for, die for, want to be my one, and no, not doing it again. I think my jaw hit the ground.

"Jessica, please come here, but meet me at our drinks." I grinned as I had just developed a game plan.

"Sir, yes, Sir."

I loved how she would do that. It was in the contract with the DORCs. While I loved the contract, I didn't love the DORCs.

Jessica met me at the kitchen island with a smile to kill all smiles that ever have smiled. Wow. I feel like my emotions are going to blow me up tonight.

As we meet at the island, I grab the ring on her collar and slowly pull her towards me. I just loved this woman so much that I wanted to cry. It's like I'd not seen her in years.

"Ma'am, you know I love you. There can be no doubt. I love you with my essence, with all I am, all I have been, and all I will ever be."

Jessica starts to tear up, not to cry but to gloss over enough to make me believe I could tip those scales if I wanted to. And I didn't. I never wanted that.

"Drink, bitch!" You'd think I was being mean, but we both laughed pretty hard at it because of how silly it was. Classic this guy. "But, there's a price to pay...."

"Sir, I don't know what's going on, but if you don't kiss me right now, I'm going to...."

And I planted one on her kisser with mine. It was sweet, tender, loving, and straightforward.

"Sir, are you OK? You seem to have...."

"I'm sorry, Ma'am. This is your chance to see me cry. I feel like I haven't seen you in a million years, that you were taken away from me by a fate, a punishment that was not fitting."

I paused, not my stupid ass pause, but because I had tears running down my cheeks. I was so happy to see her, so excited to kiss her and hold her as if I'd been somewhere else.

I grabbed a tissue and blotted my eyes and my cheeks. "Again, I'm sorry, Ma'am. I...I...I haven't seen you in such a long time, as if you were taken away from me.

"I don't know what it was that I did, but I was the one being punished by not having you. I was there, on THE OTHER SIDE, without you. I saw it. I had to live in it. It was..."

I had to go for some more tissues and blow my nose. This had gotten too real in my brain, way, way too real.

Aside from the joyousness of our collar ceremony, I'd never let Jessica see me like this. I always wanted to project a level of toughness, but this was when I couldn't do it.

"Jessica, I'm sorry you must see me like this. I mean, not to be upset, I just...."

"Sir, please let me request off the record."

"Granted."

"Punis, are you OK? In all these years, I've never seen you upset like this. What can I do for you? What do you need?"

I returned to her, never letting go of the ring on her collar. I blinked, and more tears rolled down my cheek. I'd never been this upset about anything that wasn't a cat.

"Jessica, I spent time in a world where we were not together. Where I let you walk away from me on Christmas Eve Day. We did not get one another, and it was fucking awful. It was soul-crushing."

I let go of the ring as I grabbed some more tissues, blew my nose in it, tossed the refuse, and hit some Purell on the way back.

"Sweetie, I've said this in the past, and I will say it a million more times if I have to. I waited a lifetime to meet you, I waited a lifetime to hold you, and I waited a lifetime for you to be mine.

"Jessica, you are the only thing in this world that matters to me. Period. I'm done talking about it. Get your ass back on the record, and let's drink."

"I'm sorry, Punis. Please tell me more about this place you went to. I know you've mentioned it in the past, and well... I never thought of it as being really real, just real."

Jessica paused.

"Punis, I do not doubt you. I never have, and will never, ever doubt you. Off the record or not, I love you, Punis. You are everything I have EVER wanted in another human, a million times over."

I smiled, tears slowing but feeling like I'd sinned in the contract. I hadn't, but it sure as fuck felt like that in this guy's mind.

"Jessica, I recently did a meditation where I tried to open my mind to all the goodness we create, the love we have built for one another, and how strong our bond is. But the loss of Penguin clouded that."

"I'm sorry, Punis, you know I loved him very much. He was my lap kitty for the last few years; it hurts me too. But I know it hurts you much more, and my love for you is stronger."

"Jessica, the turmoil of my soul during this session, brought me to a reality very close to ours, but the difference is Christmas Eve.

"We had the hug of all hugs; we had a wonderful conversation, but when the PA called all associates to the front, you walked away, and I did not stop you."

I got outside and talked with "Dana," as she knew the score, and she was extremely disappointed with me. How could that hug happen and I not introduce myself?

"It was my fault, Jessica, all my fault. I could have, but I didn't because I would say I disliked the idea of hitting on somebody at their job. It was bad form.

"I went back the day after Christmas, and you were not there. I asked one of the managers I'd become familiar with based on the times I shopped there, and she gave me a gut shot...."

She quickly stated, "I'm sorry, sir, she's no longer with us."

"I felt like I'd died. I'd died a million trillion times over and over in my personalized hell. Or at least like being stuck at the DMV for an eternity.

"Jessica, it tore my heart out to think I'd be nothing more to you than a smile that occasionally crossed your face. That's why you are a Sapphire....

"Jessica, while I was trapped in this reality, I was bombarded with so much pain and suffering of my own that there were so many times I was ready to...." The tears rolled down my cheeks at a faster clip.

"Jessica, without you in my life in that reality, I finally succumbed to the pain and suffering, the darkness consumed me, and I took my own life, and the boys came with me. I just wasn't strong enough to continue without you."

I could not control the tears as they poured down my face. I had just told the most important person in my world that I'd take my own life because I had let them walk away from me. I was a failure in both life and death.

"Hell, especially during 2020 and that shit show. It was so much worse to do alone. I lost my job, was out of money, and was about to lose my home. I know this is very dark.

"Jessica, I have told you this time and again; I waited a lifetime to meet you, I waited a lifetime to hold you, and I waited a lifetime for you to be mine.

"You are the greatest thing that has ever happened to me in my life. Without you, I did not have the strength to keep going; external forces were constantly crushing me."

I looked over at Jessica as I had not been directly facing her, and I could see the tears streaming down her face. This was really, REALLY not good.

Jessica turned to me and wrapped her arms around my shoulders, like on Christmas night, and told me something incredibly profound.

"Punis, I have never told you this before, but I have loved you since before Christmas night. One evening I was bagging for 'Sarah,' and I saw you in line. I switched to an open register and motioned for you to come over."

"Oh, yeah. I remember that, Jessica. But do continue."

"We didn't talk, but we stared into each other's eyes on and off, nothing out of the ordinary. But it happened after you paid and took your bags, still holding onto the handbasket.

"I believe you could see that there were many baskets behind me, and you said to me, 'Ma'am, can I take those for you and drop them off on the way out? This way, you can help this wonderful lady behind me.'

"That's when I fell in love with you, Punis. That's why I went for the hug on Christmas Eve Day. I already knew, and that was my one shot at meeting you. All of this time, I had such a crush on you."

I stood there; the tears that had dried up on my cheeks were back. I grabbed my drink and drank it in one fell swoop. That was 6 ounces of Cromulent Vodka and 6.5 oz of Zevia. Jessica's wasn't as strong, being the more standard 2 ounces.

Jessica just stared at me, not knowing what to expect. Was she supposed to follow suit? Was she to make me another drink? Was I going to say something along the lines of "Swallow that shit like a champ, bitch!"

I took a moment to try to settle myself. While that was silly, this was my one chance to get this shit under control, something I had let spiral away by allowing my emotions to be exposed. I had allowed myself to be vulnerable to Jessica.

"Jessica, I am so thankful that you told me that story. It gives me insight into you and our love I had not known about or expected. This was so sweet; it pains me."

"Punis, why would this pain you? Remember, we are still off the record here."

To be continued...

____

P18 - Unknown

Part eighteen 18, of The Jessica Files. This week, we learn more about the Unknown and what that means to this Sir and this Ma'am.

—-

This is a story of two humans who love one another like it's going out of style. They are each other's "The One." Simply stated, they love the shit out of one another.

They are so incredibly in love that they were silly enough to go into a contract life with one another and the DORCs.

————————————————————————————

Jessica and I were OK, but I was suffering from a deepening malaise. It was probably more like a giant fucking spoonful of depression due to the last conversation that Jessica and I had.

You know, the one where things broke down as I told Jessica the story of The Other Side and what happened. The emotions swept over me and provided an incredibly vulnerable instance I had tried so hard to prevent for so long.

I love Jessica. There can be no doubt. I would kill all humans for her; I would kill all humans with her. She is my absolute, like time itself. I love her, plain and simple.

I couldn't get The Other Side out of my mind. It was ever-present, like an overprotective parent who smothered the shit out of their child.

It was a real kick in the balls.

I was overwhelmed with emotions when I meditated for spiritual health and tried to rid myself of the specter of not having her.

Pain, suffering, anger. Pretty much shit that the Jedi would warn about. And these emotions were killing me, ruining me as a human and, more importantly then that, as a Dom.

I could not handle the emotions that were consuming me. I was becoming more and more, or perhaps further and further, lost in the abyss. No matter how hard I looked, I couldn't see the light to find my way home.

I can't say I wasn't taking this out on Jessica because I ultimately knew I was. I was less attentive, often waving her off when she needed something from me.

I couldn't get a grasp of the emotions that were plaguing me. It was paralyzing me, the relationship.

We had fudged things with the DORCs for a few weeks, and that was about the point at which I realized I needed to take a certain level of action.

"Jessica, get your bitch ass in here, please!" I giggled, knowing that it was classic this guy. I still loved talking shit like that. It was fun, for lack of a better word, and we would laugh.

She entered the room with a big, happy, and wide smile and said, "Sir, what do you need?"

I smiled at her. I think she knew what I was going to ask of her, but I was going to play along.

"Jessica, my love. I need you to come over here, now. And I need you to plant one on my kisser. Like you mean it. Please show me that you mean it. Make me have no doubt."

Jessica walked over to me, put her hands on my shoulders, and looked deeply and lovingly into my eyes, just like on Christmas Night many years ago.

Jessica gently kissed my forehead and said something profoundly unique: I was blown away.

Jessica stated, "Sir, I need you to wake up and return to me. I need you back here with me, Sir. I can't keep going without my Sir. You are everything to me; you are the only thing I have, Sir. Please come back to me, Punis."

And with that, I snapped out of wherever I was, whatever I was trapped in, to regain some level of consciousness and return to her. I desperately needed to feel her again, the electricity that ran through us. The kind that caused me to buy vinyl flooring.

But I woke up in a different room, a different house, perhaps as another person, as if this was a dream and I was in a Far Side comic. Alas, no such luck.

I was in yet another spinoff realm where I was lost. Another domain where I didn't have Jessica with me. I couldn't feel her. After the Christmas Night kiss, I could always feel her. That connection was so deep and magnificent that I could tell instantly when it was severed.

I was connected to her by some magical force. I think they call it LOVE.

I know the loss of Fluffle was clouding my mind, but I wasn't willing to acknowledge that as being the cause of the dark clouds that were punishing me. The type typically involved raining shit into my mind and soul and messing things up with Jessica and me.

I just wanted to go back home, back to my Jessica. Back to my boys, Shibby and Tibor. Just back to normality. And yet the prospects of that seemed so far-fetched that it made things worse. I didn't know where I was, and perhaps...

Perhaps I was on the path to getting back home. Back to Jessica and the life we had together. I had to find the way out, but I didn't know where I was. Or even when I was. That placed a massive weight on my shoulders, proverbially.

I could repeatedly hear her in my head, "Sir, I need you to wake up and come back to me," like on a loop. It was soothing and yet concerning. Again, I didn't know where I was, but I had to find my way.

And then I could hear music in the back of my head. Something familiar, something I'd heard many times, very often with Jessica. We'd put on our favorite headphones, warm up the tube amp, set the headphone splitter to equal, and sit together, listening to this band. But I couldn't remember who they were.

I started to feel like I couldn't even remember who I was, but I knew I was fighting a battle to get myself back. I didn't perceive that I was in hell or anything similar, but I knew I was in hell that was personalized for me, like being at the DMV.

I could feel the darkness that the DMV would bring to me whenever I had these feelings. Think LOTR.

228

And then I heard something so strange that I felt it pop me up and caused the sensation of an out-of-body experience. It was so weird. I couldn't see my body as if I was in some corporeal state. Nope, just felt like I was lifted out.

What I heard was so profound that I could feel myself rising increasingly into a warmer and more relaxing place. It was almost like I was ascending to heaven or something similar. I did not perceive that I was dead, but it was like that.

As I was floating upwards towards this warmth, I still could not understand the voice I was now hearing. It was garbled and pixelated, like a bad video call.

I continued on this unexpected journey until I reached what I perceived as the source of the warmth, the loving and soothing feeling that I was experiencing. This whole ordeal was confusing, enlightening, and just fucked up.

I came to, realizing I was in her lap, and she was holding me still. The scent I smelled was smelling salts, and I had been out cold, having lost consciousness. I could feel Jessica gently stroking my head. I could feel that she was holding me, the warmth that had pulled me back.

My eyes probed the room, trying to determine where I was, what the fuck was going on, and all the other variables that would go with coming to.

"Sir, are you back to me? Please, Sir, say something."

I leaned my head back a little so that I could see Jessica. To know that it was my Jessica. To ensure that I was back where I was supposed to be. I couldn't feel anything, my arms and legs were numb, and I was becoming concerned.

"Ma'am, did you call me by my given name? Over and over?"

"Yes, Sir, I did. I also cursed you out for this. But since we were still off the record, I knew I wouldn't get in trouble. But I had to do whatever I could to get you back here with me. I didn't want to lose you, Sir. I just couldn't."

"Jessica, please tell me what happened. I can't feel my arms or legs right now. What the fuck happened?"

"Sir, you had a panic attack. The worst one I've ever seen you have; it was horrific and scary. You just collapsed as if you were controlled demolition. When you fell, you hit your head pretty hard because I couldn't move fast enough to catch you."

"Well, that'd explain the headache I can feel coming on."

"Sir, I rushed and grabbed one of the anti-fatigue mats, slid it under your hips, and rolled you onto it. I then sat down on another pad, gently lifted your head into my lap, and stroked it to help you get back to me. I kept kissing your head and gently stroking your hair.

"Sir, I'm so freaked out right now. I thought I lost you."

At this point, I realized that Jessica was crying, and it wasn't a soft cry. It was the cry where you are scared of whatever event transpires, and its weight is just too much.

"Jessica, how long was I out?"

"Sir, you were out cold for about 2 minutes. And the panic attack portion, the paralysis you are feeling right now, has been...."

Jessica looked up at the clock and stated, "49 minutes and change, Sir."

Holy hell, that's incredibly concerning. And banging my head on top of it could mean concussion number 6. That will be a trip to the neurologist and a cat scan. FUCK!

I love how she was mixing my given name with our moniker, just as I had accidentally done earlier. It was cute.

"Sir, can you tell me what happened? Where did you go? Are you OK? What can I do for you right now?"

"Ma'am, I'm not sure, but I'd like to discuss it later once I have processed all of this. I will share it with you, on or off the record; I swear on our lives and that of the boys.

"Jessica, because of this journey to the other side, I will be able to finish writing about the darkness and what the other side brought to me.

"When it's printed, I will give you the first copy, and you will finally know the absolute truth of how much I love you."

I paused. "I think it will make for a good story."
____

Epilogue

Part nineteen 19 of The Jessica Files. This week, we learn more about the redemption of this Sir and this Ma'am.

—-

Following some of the recent events of our most excellent couple, Punis and Jessica were in dire need of something to bring them back together.

————————————————————————————————————

I woke up sometime following the events of the Great Panic Attack. But this time, it was a bit different. In this instance, I was lying on my back with Jessica's head on my chest; her arm draped over my thorax.

This was new and, in some regards, welcomed, given the recent events in our lives.

At this point, Jessica was still off the record, and I had to get her back into compliance. While it would not be hard, I had to be sure we were past this part.

That was so important to me; I did not want to hear from the DORCs. One time would be too many, given my feelings about the whole "Testing" thing when renewals come around.

There was this one hidden gem in the contract but exceptionally buried in the pages, as a mere afterthought or some mustard stain you find way too late, something like that.

I loved when I'd get to say to Jessica, "I grant you off the record."

I think that's a turn-on phrase for me. If I recall correctly, I didn't have Jessica in my life for less than a year before she was collared as mine, inside and out.

Sometimes, I just wanted to hear what Jessica had to say or what she was thinking. Such an intelligent and thoughtful human, far brighter than anyone thought. She was brilliant.

Off the record, what a little gem. Oh, man, did I ever love it when I could recognize the look and work us towards that moment? To be honest, 95% of the time, something blew that spot up.

Jessica had to live within the context of the contract. We all did. It did not matter who it was that was the Dom and sub; the rules were the rules.

I don't mean to be an ass but don't sign a contract if you aren't going to honor it. Seems like too much effort for no reason.

"Punis, why would this pain you? Remember, we are still off the record here."

"Jessica, we need to get back on the record. There's too much of a time gap right now, and the folks at the DORCs will be all over our shit."

I've never run afoul of the DORCs, and I've always never wanted to either. Too many horror stories within the community for anyone not to take their contracts seriously... One day I will detail some of those in another chapter.

The DORCs will sue the shit out of you. I suppose that's less will and more always do. I'd rather not deal with that, and I'd rather not subject Jessica to that, either.

That's why Jessica and I always ensured that we stayed within the rules and regulations outlined in our contracts, including the frequency and accuracy of our filings.

She knew that was the truth, but the power pulled on her like something from The Hobbit or The Lord of the Rings.

"Jessica, I love you. If you disagree with my request, I will have to Section 14 you. And that would not be lovely like you are."

Jessica looked at me; I've long felt she was weighing her odds or trying to recall what that meant. I knew that meant forced compliance, and I did not want the forced part.

"Jessica, like you called me to come back to you previously, I need you to come back to me as my sub. I need that, Ma'am. We need that."

"Sir, I'd like to go back on the record, please."

"Yes, Ma'am, we are back on the record."

"Sir, are you OK?"

"Ma'am, I owe my life and existence to you, your love, your thoughtfulness, your instinct to save me. Your love, your heart, that saved us from destruction.

"Jessica, it will be known to the DORCs that you, and you alone, saved all of us. Those are the facts; I know that to be true.

"Jessica, on the record or not, you saved me. You saved the boys. You saved me from a potential health scare. There is nothing I can do in our world to say thank you more than this.

"Jessica, not to sound like a broken record, but you are singularly the greatest, most influential, astounding, and spectacular thing that has ever happened to me. You are the one constant that I have wanted in my life."

I trailed off, not knowing what to say given the sheer amount of praise I'd thrown down here.

She indeed was that important to me. Without her, I'd have been left at the DMV, a purgatory by another name.

____

ACKNOWLEDGEMENTS

Never in my life had I ever imagined that I would write a book. Up until two years ago, the longest thing I'd ever written was about three pages. That was until my friend and mentor, **The Reverend CD**, challenged me to write more.

Without you, CD, nothing I have written or have yet to write, none of that would be possible if not for you. If not for that visit to the cemetery, our conversation, and how it made me think.

You are most excellent, so much so that you are the first person and sometimes the only person to read the material I've written over the last two-plus years. That covers blogs, books, and pamphlets for underprivileged reindeer.

You have been there with me when I was heading towards the gates of hell and have been the hand that pulled me back. You, and only you, have done so.

You have inspired me time and again, and you are the most influential and important person in my life in all the combined years.

You are special to me as a friend, and you damn well know I consider you a part of my family. I love you, good sir; there can be no doubt.

——

" **Fry**" - Besties be Besties. Thank you for all of the support you have given me. I wish I was half as good as a human, as a friend, that you have been to me.

Thank you for never discouraging me from writing this, even though it was a shit show of long, crazy... oh wait, it still is. I hope you similarly help me wherever my writing takes us, you have such a phenomenal mind.

And as my best friend for many years and through so many trials and tribulations, I love you as my brother. You know this to be true.

——

The Great Daniel L., You are a supremely talented artist, one whom I trust implicitly, and you know this to be true. You are also one of the few who knew about any projects I have, am, and will work on.

I also hope you know how proud of you that I am. I am honored to be your client and share parts of my life with you.

Thank you for listening to these stories over the years, even if they were scattered and told two hours at a time.

———————————————————————————————

Oh, **Andrea**, where could I possibly start? You are such a fantastic person, someone who has known the multiplicity of this guy. The complexity of having been the OG Sapphire and someone in and around my life for so fucking long.

You said something recently while we were talking, noting that we've known one another for over one-half of our lives, 25 years now. I was blown away.

I owe you so much. Thank you for being a friend.
Thank you for the OG "ass walking away moment."
Thank you for knowing the most important things
in life and their value over another

Thank you for reading these works to me and for
telling me what's what. I have always appreciated
your candor, thoughtfulness, and drawl.

————————————————————————————

Doctor G - Thank you, you have helped me
become me. No one could do what you have done
for me as a human, slowly developing me into a
slightly less fucked up version of myself, even if it
has taken nearly 20 years.

Your patience, kindness, and love have saved me
more than I can count. I thank you immensely for
being there for me, human to human, so many times
over many years.

————————————————————————————

Good Sister - Thank you. You have saved me twice. Nothing I do and no amount of money I could give you could ever say thank you like this. I would never have been able to create this if you hadn't saved me.

I would have been stuck there, on the other side, suffering an all too similar fate.

I will only have two sisters, and we know this to be true.
____

Bad Sister - I surely couldn't thank Good Sister without thanking you but in a much different way. You have always been good to me from the moment I came into this world. You have never done me wrong.

I know this isn't something I would usually say, but I wanted to say in a published book, "I love you. You are an excellent sister, and I am proud to be your brother."

I will only have two sisters, and we know this to be true.
____

Mrs. B - You have been to hell and back, and my hand is outstretched to you. You have dealt with massive pain and strife, and my hand is outstretched to you. You have endured, and my hands celebrate you, your strength, and the drive you have.

I am so thankful to have you in my life for so long for two reasons. First, you called me that night, worried and empathetic, knowing I had lost so much. Second, I am thankful for that birthday chat we had many years ago.

I wish I could do more to get you where you need to be, but I can only show you the love and support you have given me over the last 15+ years.

You, your most handsome husband, and Charlie are amazing. You know this to be true.

————————————————————————————————

Ms. J - You are such an enigma to me, even after so many years as friends. Thank you for poking fun at this story and developing "The Department of Rules and Contracts" or DORCs with me.

248

I could say so many things, but more than everything, I will always cherish you, our friendship, and the drunken handholding walks.

———————————————————————————————

"**Dana**" - There is no part of me that will never love you as a friend. You were there with me and experienced this story. You virtually held my hand and tried to guide this idiot. I'm sorry that I failed and went to the other side.

Without you, "**Dana**," this story would never be told. "**Dana**," without you, I'd never of lived to see "The Hello Hello Game" or the funniest of anything related to this story, #ISHBU. (See TJF2 for that shit)

I miss your Christmas cookie massacre silliness and all the fun things friends do. You are a magnificent human and will be even more astonishing as a Mom. I am so proud of you.

Thank you for being my friend, the first FLA, and rebuilding the right things in life. I'll always be thankful for all the fantastic things you brought to my life.

"**Dana**," I can say this a million times over, something that **The Great Daniel L.**, as well as **Doctor G,** both know to be true; while they got to hear the story one or two hours at a time, you lived through that with me in near real-time, and I owe you such a debt that, like **Good Sister**, I can never repay.

———————————————————————————

And lastly... **<u>Sapphire</u>** - I will be here, waiting for you on the other side.

After all, this is a love story...